Seth & Greyson

By Jessica Sorensen

D1469047

For information:

jessicasorensen.com

Cover Design and Photography: Mae I Design

www.maeidesign.com

Seth & Greyson (The Coincidence, #7)

ISBN: 978-1500733834

Chapter 1

Seth

I've never been a fan of school, yet here I am, arriving early to my freshman year at the University of Wyoming. It was either begin summer semester or stay home until fall. Living under my mother's roof and her rules, like no dating in the public eye, made the choice really easy. My mother believes the opinions of the residents of Mapleville actually matter, and I've never completely understood why. Mapleville is a tiny town in the middle of nowhere with a population of maybe a thousand tops. It's a blip on a map that most people don't know exists, and a place I hope to forget, mainly because it's where I got the cast on my arm.

The cast. Another reason my mother didn't want me dating, and why she was relieved I chose to start college at the beginning of summer.

But the cast wasn't the only reason I chose to bail out of a boring summer in Mapleville. I never felt like I be-longed in a place where dressing in clothes stylish enough to be in high fashion magazines caused people to gawk at you like you were strolling about in your underwear.

Despite being more than ready to escape my past and take this leap, standing in front of the historical main entrance to the campus, watching students hurrying in and out as if they know exactly where they're going... I'm completely overwhelmed and I feel so... lost.

Reminding myself that this is my fresh start and to take it one step at a time, I sling my backpack over my shoulder and start up the stairs toward the glass doors. The sun shining in the clear blue sky and the temperature probably pushing one hundred *almost* make me question dressing in designer jeans, boots, and a button-down shirt with the sleeves rolled up, but I look so fantastic I can't completely regret it.

I wind through the hallway, searching the room numbers until I find the door to my Pre-Calculus class. I smile to myself as I walk in, trying to be the sparkling person I was before the *incident*, hoping maybe a cheerful appearance will equal fast friendships.

Right away, I can tell the summer classes have a lower attendance because I'm already pushing being late and there are a total of ten people seated. Skimming my options, I pick a spot in the back next to a mousy looking girl with short brown hair and the saddest eyes I've ever seen.

After what I went through back at my old school, I'm careful about the people I surround myself with. If I'm not, I could end up in the same situation that put this damn cast on my arm. I only have one good arm left and don't think I can take any more breaks.

As the professor comes strolling into the classroom, I use my good hand to unzip my bag and dig out the textbook. I relax back in the seat and stare out the window as the professor begins rambling through the introduction, then passes out the syllabus.

Eventually, I notice the girl glance in my direction, and I offer her a smile. Her eyes widen and her attention whips back to the paper she's doodling on. I can't quite put my finger on why, but I feel an urge to befriend her. There's something about her that reminds me of myself, like she's trying to hide herself behind baggy clothes and a God-awful haircut. Granted, I would never, *ever* wear anything that hideous, but I get the whole trying-to-hide-who-you-really-are part. I did it for years before saying to hell with it. A few months later, I was beat up, but I wouldn't go back and change my decision. Living a lie wasn't any easier.

I lean to the side and whisper to the girl, "It's okay. I'm not going to bite." I extend my hand to her. "My name's Seth."

"I-I'm Callie," she stammers, reaching to take my hand.

But she tenses at the very last second and quickly withdraws, putting her hands on her lap.

"It's nice to meet you, Callie." I study her with curiosity, trying to figure out if it's just me she's afraid of or people in general. When I walked into the classroom, she was seated as far away from everyone as possible and I wonder if maybe that move was on purpose. "Can I borrow a pencil?"

Nodding, she digs one out of her bag and kind of tosses it at me before wiping her palms on her jeans and fixing her attention on taking notes.

I learn a total of nada for the day, and when I read through the syllabus, I question whether I'll survive torturous Pre-Cal. The numbers and formulas already have my head spinning and my attention drifting to what outfit I'll wear tomorrow instead of the assignment.

Seth & Greyson

I'm in a daze packing up and making my way out of the classroom, but snap out of it when I spot the girl scrambling to get the hell out of Dodge. At the doorway, she nearly crashes into some guy, and just about comes unglued. Shaking with fear, she stutters an apology and hurries down the hallway, surprisingly fast for being so tiny.

Interesting. I definitely want to find out what her deal is.

I have one more class for the day, which doesn't seem like a huge workload, but I'm exhausted by the time I return to my dorm. My roommate's not there, which isn't a big shocker. I think I made him uncomfortable the day we met when I complimented him on his hair. He's pretty much been MIA ever since.

I lamely start a few assignments then fall asleep around nine o'clock. For the next seven days, I'm stuck in the droning pattern, going to school, doing homework, looking for a job, then dozing off early. Eighteen years old, and I feel as ancient as my grandparents, who believe the day ends when the sun goes down. Seriously, with the way they act, you'd think they believed in vampires.

On day eight, I grow restless and bored. If I'm going to have any fun while at college—and I made a promise to myself that I would—then I'm going to have to make some friends. Ones I can have a good time with. Ones who will accept me for who I am. Ones I can trust. Ones who maybe need me just as much as I need them so I don't come off all needy.

The problem is, outside of the quiet girl who sits next to me in Pre-Cal, I haven't talked to anyone since I moved to Laramie, and most of our conversations consist of me yammering and her nodding.

During class today, I thrum my fingers against the desk while plotting how to make the skittish girl open up to me. I don't know why I'm so dead set on making friends with her—she's probably the most difficult person to carry on a conversation with. Maybe that's the reason. Perhaps I'm so bored that I'm dying for a challenge.

"So, do you get anything the professor's talking about?" I ask toward the end of class.

She stares down at the book with a pencil gripped in her hand. "Not really."

"Me, neither. Isn't math so boring?"

She nods, but remains quiet. I rack my mind for something to say to her.

"So, you're a freshman right?" I ask after class is dismissed.

She stuffs her book into her bag, nods, and then scurries for the door.

"Wait," I call out, rushing after her. "Do you have another class to go to today?"

She pauses in the doorway and shakes her head without looking at me. "No, I-I'm going back to my dorm."

I stop beside her. "And doing what?"

She peeks up at me, and I can tell by her widened eyes that she's terrified. "Studying."

I rake my fingers through my honey blond hair. "That sounds... Well, extremely boring. Don't you want to do something, I don't know, more adventurous?"

"Not really. And homework is fitting since I'm a pretty boring person." For a faltering moment, amusement flashes in her eyes.

Hmmm... under her oversized jeans and t-shirt, I think she actually might have a sense of humor.

"Well, I'm not a boring person. Trust me." I press my hand to my chest. "I'm actually pretty fabulous and fun, but I've been kind of a dud the last week. I think it might be the combo of school and summer. The two are like socks and sandals—they're never supposed to go together."

Her gaze flicks across my black jeans and grey t-shirt topped by a plaid button-up before she wraps her arms around herself, like she's suddenly embarrassed of her clothes. "Well, it was nice talking to you, but I have to go." She starts out the doorway.

"Hey, you want to go get some coffee?" I stroll down the hallway beside her. "I've been dying to try out this little café on the corner."

She swiftly shakes her head. "I can't."

"Why not?"

"Because I'm busy."

"With your homework?" I ask with a hint of amusement.

"Yes, with my homework." She doesn't sound angry, just nervous.

When we reach the end of the hall, she pushes open the exit doors and we step outside into the sunlight and the fairly mellow campus yard. She immediately veers left and makes a beeline for the tree area to the side of the main entrance.

"Come on. Just one cup of coffee." I follow after her. "I'm super bored and I really don't want to go back to my dorm yet. My roommate likes to leave half-eaten bags of chips and soda cans everywhere, along with his dirty underwear. Plus, the room reeks of cheese."

She scrunches up her nose. "Why cheese?"

I shrug. "I have no idea where the smell is coming from, and that's part of the problem."

Her face twists in disgust, but a spark of a smile touches her lips.

"So, what do you say?" I smile. "Will you help me escape the mysteriously smelling room for an hour?"

She halts on the sidewalk and looks at me for the first time since we started talking. "Just for coffee, right?"

I shrug. "Maybe. Although, I have to warn you that when I get bored, I can get really spastic. And I've been bored for about a week now."

She shifts her weight. "Okay…" She bites her lip nervously. "But it's not like a… date, right?"

I snort a laugh and quickly cover my mouth with my hand. When her expression plummets and her cheeks turn pink, I realize how bad that must have came off.

"I didn't mean it like that," I quickly say. "Under all those God-awful clothes, I can tell you're a beautiful girl." I wonder how far I should go with this. I haven't really opened up to anyone since the *incident*, but it'll come out sooner or later if we're going to be friends. "But you're not really my type, seeing as how you're not a guy."

It takes her a moment to catch up with me. "Oh." Her stiff posture suddenly relaxes. "That's good. I mean, that you like guys." She stumbles over her words then rolls her eyes at herself. "Sorry, I'm just really glad you weren't hitting on me." She smiles at me. "We can go get coffee."

"Fantastic." I smile, hoping to figure out more of what the hell is behind her squirrely behavior. "Can I ask, though, why you were so wigged out when you thought I was hitting on you?"

She lifts her shoulder and gives a half-shrug, her lips remaining fastened.

Okaaaay. This friendship might be more difficult than I thought. Good thing I love a good challenge.

Seth & Greyson

"So Callie, other than running away from potential dates, what do you like to do for fun?" I ask as we hike down the sidewalk toward the café on the corner.

"Nothing, really." She slides the strap of the bag higher on her shoulder. "Other than write. What about you?"

"Well, I love a lot of things, like dancing, partying, going to the movies. But my real passion is clothes, which is pretty obvious."

She casts a self-conscious glance at her outfit. "It sounds like we're pretty much opposites."

"Which can make for a fabulous friendship," I say. When she gives me a wary glance, I add, "Ever heard the saying that opposites attract?" I stop at the corner of the street and hammer my thumb against the crosswalk button. "But because I'm, well *me*, I have to ask. What's up with the baggy clothes?"

She stares at the quaint café just across the street. "I just don't like standing out."

"Okay…I don't mean to be rude or anything, but while your look would have totally rocked the nineties, we're way past the grunge and baggy pants fad, so it kind of makes you stand out like a disco ball in a Goth club."

She tucks a strand of her hair behind her ear and glances at me. "I've been wearing this same look since forever... for my own reasons." She hugs her arms around herself. "It's all I'm comfortable in, and I'm too afraid if I start wearing other stuff, I'll feel unsafe."

The word *unsafe* sends off warning bells in my head. I remember how safe I felt with my ex-boyfriend Braiden until he snatched it away. I've been trying my best to keep going, keep being me, and fight to get the feeling of comfort and security back, but sometimes it gets hard, especially at night when I have to close my eyes and dream.

"Why would you feel unsafe?" I ask, leaning against the street post.

Her jaw clenches. "For a lot of reasons."

I wonder if those reasons played into her panic when she thought I was asking her out.

I stare down at the bright blue, doodle-covered cast on my arm. "Sometimes, I feel unsafe walking around in my own skin, too, but then I think about how unfair it is for me to pretend to be someone else and honestly, how fucking boring it is not being me." I flash her a grin.

Seth & Greyson

A soft giggle escapes her lips. She's so shocked by the sound that I question how long it's been since she's laughed.

"You know what?" she asks as we start across the street. "I think you were right about the opposites attract thing. I think..." She considers her words. "I think you could be a good friend for me."

"Oh, honey, I'm going to be the most amazing friend you've ever had," I say as I hop onto the curb.

"I have to warn you, I haven't had many friends." She steps onto the curb with me. "So *Most Amazing Friend* is a pretty easy title to win."

"Honestly, I haven't had that many, either," I tell her as we cross the parking lot. "And I pretty much lost all of them when I..." I glance down at my arm as my thoughts drift back to my past.

"What happened?" she asks, pulling open the door to the café.

"It's a long, painful story," I reply as I step inside. The scent of fresh coffee and baked goods fills my nostrils and I breathe it in.

"Mine, too," she says as we move for the counter. "I mean, the story of why I wear these clothes is."

I glance up at the menu to figure out what to order, but quickly look back at her when an idea pops into my head.

"How about this," I say. "I'll tell you mine if you tell me yours."

Her head angles to the side as she considers my offer. "It might take some time for me to tell you everything, but if you're willing to be patient, then you have yourself a deal."

Patience has never been my strong suit, but I like the idea of having someone to share my story with. I just hope I can trust her.

I stick out my hand and she hesitantly takes it. "All right, Callie. You have yourself a deal. And a brand new best friend."

Chapter 2

Three Months later...

Seth

"God, it's like spazzville around here today," I remark to Callie while scrunching my nose at the freshmen scrambling around the campus yard. I wait for her to join in on the fun of mocking our student body, but, as usual, Callie has dazed off. "Are you spacing off on me again?"

She blinks her attention to me and playfully nudges me in the shoulder. "Now don't be arrogant. Just because we both decided to do the summer semester and we know where everything is, doesn't make us better than them."

"Uh, yeah, it kind of does." I roll my eyes at her absurd logic. "We're like upper class freshmen."

She sips her coffee to hide her smile, something only I seem able to bring out. "You know there's no such thing as an upper class freshman."

I sigh, running my fingers through my lightly tousled hair. "Yeah, I know, especially for people like you and me. We're like two black sheep."

Which might be the truest statement I've ever said. Over the last three months, I've learned a lot about Callie and just how traumatic her past was. Raped by her older brother's friend at twelve, Callie has spent the years since then hiding what happened and building a shell around herself, cloaking herself in ugly, baggy clothes and isolating herself from her friends until she had none left. I've made it my mission the last few months to push her out of her shell.

Yeah, she's still a work in progress. I have yet to get her to wear a dress, shorts, or anything remotely tight enough to show off her petite figure. I'm working on it, though.

"There are many more black sheep out there than just you and me," she disagrees with me, as she typically does. "And I've toned it down. I'm even wearing a red t-shirt today, like the list said to do."

My lips quirk. "Which would look even better if you'd let those pretty locks of yours down, instead of hiding them in that ponytail all the time."

Seth & Greyson

"One step at a time," she says. "It was hard enough just letting my hair grow out. It makes me feel weird. Besides, that has yet to be added to the list."

Aw, the infamous list, one of my most brilliant drunken plans. After a night of one too many shots of vodka, we confessed our darkest secrets and then I decided that we should make a list of things we're most afraid to do. Over the last couple of months, we've been gradually working to cross items off.

"Well, it needs to be. In fact, I'm doing it when I get back to my room. Plus, you're still wearing that God-awful hoodie," I say, tugging on the bottom of her ratty grey jacket. "I thought we talked about that hideous thing. That you're beautiful and you don't need to cover up. Besides, it's like eighty degrees outside."

She wraps the jacket around herself. "Subject change, please."

I swing my arm around her and sigh, but give her exactly what she asks. "Fine, but one day we're going to talk about a complete makeover, which I will supervise."

She sighs heavily. "We'll see."

Her Debby Downer attitude is ruining my mood. As

21

her best friend, it's my job to cheer her up.

I slam to a halt and whirl around in front of her. "I just have to say one more thing." I place a finger to the corner of her eye. "I like the maroon eyeliner much better than the excessive black."

"I have your approval on that." She presses her hand dramatically to her heart, a gesture she picked up from me. "I'm so relieved. It's been weighing on my mind since this morning."

I roll my eyes as I smile. "You're doing good in every department, I just wish you'd wear a dress or shorts or something for once and show off those legs of yours."

Her expression instantly sinks. "Seth, you know why… I mean, you know… I can't…"

"I know. I'm just trying to be encouraging."

"I know you are and that's why I love you."

I want to hug her for saying that. It's been a long time since anyone has said that they loved me. Even my mother has taken to a formal, "I'm glad you're okay. Talk to you later. Bye," whenever we talk on the phone.

"You're so much happier than when I first met you." I tuck a strand of her hair behind her ear. "I wish you could be this way around everyone, Callie. That you would stop hiding from everyone. It's sad no one gets to see how great you are."

"And vice-versa," she says, understanding me better than anyone ever has.

Attempting to lighten the mood, I smirk and ask, "What do you think? Should we hit up one of the tours and make fun of the tour guide?"

"You know the way to my heart."

We stroll up the sidewalk under the shade of the trees and make our way to the entrance. Everyone is in a state of panic, trying to figure out where to go. I watch the scatter-brained people, fully entertained as they trip over their own feet and grow frustrated when they take the wrong way.

Through my twisted internal laughter, one guy in particular catches my attention. He's standing in the stairway with a middle-aged woman and man who I'm guessing are his parents. A tad on the tall side, he's wearing black jeans and a grey, long-sleeved shirt, an outfit that screams dark and edgy, which is a bit of a contrast to my blunt and bold. Still, he's hot as hell with the most gorgeous eyes I've ever seen and sandy blonde hair that looks absolutely touchable. A rush of terrifying excitement ripples through my body.

It's been a while since I've felt this attracted to someone. This guy has my adrenaline pumping to the point where I'm actually starting to sweat.

Callie says something beside me and I nod, even though I have honest to God no idea what she said. My eyes are locked on the guy as he leans in and gives his mother a hug before moving to his father. When he turns away, his eyes catch mine from across the crowd. I should probably look away. I don't know him and have no clue as to his sexual orientation, so openly gawking definitely *isn't* me being careful. But his lips tug to a half-smile and I'm pulled in.

Just. Like. That.

"Holy sexiness," I mutter under my breath.

"Heads up," someone yells from close by.

I jerk my attention back to Callie just in time to see a solid guy with brown hair slam right into her.

"Holy shit." I slap my hand over my mouth as my tiny Callie falls flat on her back.

Not only does she look hurt, but I can tell the contact is sending her into a panic.

"Get off of me," she yells as she wiggles to get out

from under him. "Get off of me now!"

I bend over to help her up, but the guy quickly pushes off her and Callie scrambles to stand up.

"I'm so sorry," the guy says, looking genuinely apologetic. "I didn't see you there."

Callie blinks, clearly in a state of shock. "Kayden?"

My eyes snap wide. "Holy shit."

The infamous Kayden Owens, a guy from Callie's hometown. Callie stepped in to help Kayden one night right before she came to Laramie, stopping his father from beating the shit out of him. That story made me love her even more, and I secretly wished that she had lived in Mapleville so she could have done the same thing for me.

She abruptly snatches hold of my hand, dragging me toward the entrance, and I suddenly remember Mr. Sexy Eyes. My gaze darts to the stairway, but my mood plummets when I can't find him anywhere.

Callie grips onto me as she steers us inside, letting go as she leans against the wall, struggling to regain her composure. "That was Kayden Owens," she says between deep breaths.

My eyes wander back towards the grassy courtyard,

where Kayden stands talking to a hot guy who looks like he's got his panties in a bunch. "*The* Kayden Owens. The one you saved, right?"

"I didn't save him." She bites on her thumbnail. "I just interrupted something."

"Something that was about to get ugly."

"Anyone would've done the same." She tries to walk off, but I grab her elbow and pull her back.

She's not getting away that easy. She needs to understand exactly how amazing she is.

"No, a lot of people would've walked by," I tell her. "It's a common fact that a lot of people will turn their heads in the other direction. I know this from experience."

My heart tightens in my chest and for a faltering moment, I'm back in the dirt with fists and feet flying at me. The air smells like hate and in the center of the violence, my body aches.

"I'm sorry you had to go through that," she says softly.

"Don't be sorry, Callie. You have your own sad story."

Offering me a sympathetic smile, we start down the hallway toward a line forming in front of a table stacked with neon pink flyers and pamphlets and plates full of baked goods.

"He didn't even recognize you." I shove my way through the crowd to the front of the line and snatch up a pink flyer, along with two cookies. Sugar cookies. My fave.

"He barely acknowledged me, ever." She shakes her head when I offer her a cookie.

"Well, he should recognize you now." I nibble on a stale cookie. "You did save his ass from getting beat."

"It's not that big a deal," she says, shrugging me off. "Now, can we please change the subject to something else?"

It's the second time she's asked me that today, and I decide it's probably time to give her a break.

Finishing off the rest of the cookie, I link arms with her and spin around, stopping abruptly when I slam into someone so hard it knocks the wind from me.

"Jesus." I step back, scowling overdramatically.

When I see who I ran into, though, annoyance turns to *holy shit my skin is on fire.* Because Mr. Sexy Eyes in all is hotness is standing in front of me, rubbing his forehead.

"Sorry about that," I quickly apologize, quickly checking him out. "I wasn't watching where I was going."

"It's okay. It was kind of my fault... I wasn't watching where I was going, either." He lowers his hand to his side and his gaze flicks between Callie and me, slowly calculating something before offering a lopsided smile.

I return his smile, but can't think of anything to say. It's been so long since I've flirted that even thinking about doing so sends me back to that night. I can almost feel the grit of the dirt in my mouth, can almost taste the foul tang of blood.

Choosing a course that's completely out of character for me, I seal my lips shut and walk around him.

"Dude, we both must be cursed today," Callie says as we push our way through the mob.

"Cursed?" I ask, still slightly distracted over what happened with the sexy stranger. I already wish I could have a do-over, go back and say something. It's been way, way too long since I flirted and I really do miss it.

"Yeah, with running into people."

"Oh, yeah, right." I barely comprehend what she said, my thoughts instead swirling over the guy, who he is, whether he's a freshman, if he's thinking about me like I'm completely obsessing over him.

I think about him a lot through freshman orientation, but unfortunately don't see him again. Maybe it's for the best. I'm still a little iffy on whether I'm ready to try dating again. Plus, I don't know if this guy is available or even interested. He looked like he was interested, but I don't know for sure.

Besides, the cast only came off weeks ago and the wounds and scars are still as fresh as the memory behind them.

Chapter 3

Greyson

I've always considered myself pretty lucky. I've had a good life, filled with mostly happy memories, and I have two of the most supportive parents. Still, I struggle with coming out of my shell. I'm not shy or anything, but I'm not the chattiest person, either. It makes it difficult to start freshman year at a college clear across the country from where I grew up, but after receiving a photography scholarship from the University of Wyoming, I decided to give a new location a try, embark on a new adventure.

After spending my first weekend cooped up in the one-bedroom apartment my parents helped me rent, I've started to question whether I made the right choice.

"You sound homesick, sweetie" my mother says over the phone. "Darn it. I'm not sure if I can think of anything you can take to cure it."

Seth & Greyson

I bite back a chuckle. My parents are very hippy-ish and my mother is a huge believer in herbal remedies. She's a self-proclaimed artist/tarot card reader and my dad's an herbalist. Their quirky, offbeat personalities have made my life interesting, to say the least.

"That's okay." I pull the tape off a box—I'm still working on unpacking. "I think I might need to cure this one all on my own."

"Well, just don't forget to smile," she says. "A smile can fix so much."

I unfold the top of the box. "I'm smiling right now. I swear."

"Good. And if you need anything, you know you can call me. Day or night. I don't want you getting lonely."

"I'm fine. In fact, I'm getting ready to head off to my first class and I have a feeling I'm going to make some new friends there."

"That's so weird because I had a dream last night that you made three new friends today. One was in English class, so keep your eyes open."

I shake my head as I wander back to my room to get dressed. "All right, Mom, I'll make sure to keep a lookout."

"Good. Call me tonight and let me know if I was right."

"Sounds good."

"And promise me you won't go into your shell. I know you don't mind being alone, but I don't want you missing out on opportunities to make new friends and maybe date a little bit. You haven't even mentioned a boy since Carter. I hope he didn't break your heart."

"He didn't break my heart," I assure her, which is the truth. My heart has never been broken because I've never been in love. When it comes to dating, I've been a casual fling kind of guy, something I never really thought much about until Carter broke things off because he said I was too closed off. It kind of opened my eyes to how my stoicism comes off, but breaking the habit hasn't been easy and I'm still getting my footing. But it's been so long since I've gotten any or even went out with anyone that I'm starting to get a little sexually frustrated. "And I promise I won't go into my shell or whatever it is you called it."

"Say it like you mean it," she insists. "I want to hear the excitement in your voice."

Seth & Greyson

I pull open the dresser drawer and dig through my clothes for a shirt. "Okay! I promise!" I say with forced cheer as I roll my eyes. "There. Better?"

"Much better. I love you, sweetie."

"Love you, too."

I hang up and blow out a breath. While my mom has complete faith that her dream is going to come true, I'm skeptical she's seen my future as she so often claims to do. Besides, I'm really nervous, which usually means I'll come off awkward and unapproachable, the quiet, tortured artist who broods at the back of the class.

After I get dressed in a grey t-shirt and a dark pair of jeans, I slip on my black boots, grab my bag, and head out the door. The apartment I live in is a ways from the campus. I'm hoping by next semester I can find a closer place, but for now, I make do and use the five-mile walk as an excuse for exercise. On my way, I grab my camera from my bag and take snapshots of an awesome looking Victorian house and then a few streets where the blossom trees canopy over the asphalt. Back in Florida, we didn't really have four seasons and I find it fascinating to watch the leaves falling from the trees. I walk by a few people who grab my attention, mainly because they either look intense, sad, or extremely happy, and I covertly take pictures of them as I pass. I have a thing with capturing emotion in my pictures and seek them out wherever I go.

By the time I reach the busy campus yard, I've probably taken at least a hundred pictures. Looking through the lens, I zoom around the grassy area just to the side of the university's main building, looking for the perfect shot. Angling the camera at one of the benches where two people are sitting, I pause.

The guy and girl are huddled together, as if they've carved their own private world for each other. The guy says something, swinging his hands around animatedly, and the girl busts up laughing, throwing her head back. The guy smiles at this, seeming happy that he made his friend laugh. He jumps to his feet, grabs her arm, and spins her around and around until she almost falls down.

There's such freedom in the way they talk and laugh, overwhelming happiness to the point that I actually start to feel happy just observing them. I consider going over there and introducing myself. Why the hell not? It won't hurt anything and it's not like I haven't introduced myself to complete strangers before. Besides, the guy looks familiar. As they wander up the path, the guy directly faces me. I get a full view of his golden blonde hair and gorgeous brown eyes, realizing I've definitely seen him before. It's the guy that was staring at me earlier this week.

Everything about him, from his eccentric taste in clothes, to the way he entertains his friend, to the confidence in his walk screams *Notice Me!* And fuck, do I notice him, so much that I go all stalker and snap at least twenty pictures of him. I only put the camera down when he and the girl he's with disappear inside the main building.

Putting the camera back into my bag, I hurry off to English class. As I sit down in a desk toward the back of the room, I try not to think about what my mother said this morning, but I find myself assessing each person as they enter.

It's not until the object of my stalking walks through the doorway that I consider maybe my crazy mother was right. I quickly realize how insane that would make me for believing her and force myself to stop thinking like my mother. I've always been more levelheaded than both my parents, and I want to hold onto the trait.

Tearing my attention away from him, I lean over to grab my textbook and a pen out of my bag. When I sit up, I'm surprised to find he's taken the desk right next to mine.

Up close, he's even better looking, but there's a hint of nervousness in his eyes that I didn't notice while looking through the lens, which is kind of strange. Usually, I see more when I'm taking pictures. Or maybe he was just happier when he was around his friend.

"Hey," he greets me with a slightly nervous smile.

"Hey." I rack my brain for something to say that won't make me sound awkward, but he beats me to the punch.

"I'm Seth," he says, extending his hand to me.

"Greyson." I take his hand, noting it shakes a little in mine. "Is this your first class?"

"For the fall semester, yeah."

"You're not a freshman?"

"No, I am," he replies. "I just started the year this summer."

I smile, and decide to flirt a little, see where it goes. "So you should be a pro at classes by now."

"You would think so," he muses. "But I'm not a fan of school and being a fantastic student is at the bottom of my list, right between getting a good night's rest and becoming friends with my slobbish roommate."

Seth & Greyson

"You live in the dorm?" I ask and he nods. "I actually thought about doing that, but my parents insisted I need a place of my own. That it's good for my aura."

His brow cocks. "Aura?"

"Yeah, they're a little crazy like that, but in a good way." I try to pick up on the vibe he's giving. Is he just being friendly? Or is he interested in me?

I watch as his eyes trail down over my neck and chest, suddenly realizing that we're still holding hands. Definitely a bit awkward, but in a good way. And that means he's interested, right?

When his gaze reaches our joined hands, he startles and quickly pulls away. I catch a flash of alarm in his eyes as he scans the room before looking back at me.

He clears his throat. "So, you just moved here?"

I wonder why he's acting so weird suddenly. Maybe I misread his interest. Doubtful, though, so what is it? "Yeah, from Florida."

His eyes snap wide. "Holy shit. How the hell did you end up going from the sunshine state to cowboy central?"

"Is Wyoming cowboy central? I thought that was Texas?"

"Clearly, you haven't been around when the fair rolls in. It's like rodeo central. Nothing but cowboy hats, boots, and ridiculously tight pants as far as the eye can see."

"Sounds... interesting, I guess."

"Try horrifying. Some of the stuff I've seen through those tight jeans," he shudders, "still haunts my nightmares."

I laugh at him and he grins, obviously pleased with himself. Like how he was with the girl earlier, he seems to enjoy making people laugh.

I consider what my mom said about finding friends and going out on dates. He's hot, nice, and funny. As long as I can keep the conversation going and find the right moment, I might ask him out. Get myself out of the damn rut I've been in.

"So, I was thinking..." I trail off as a larger guy wearing a jersey sits down in the desk in front of me and Seth swiftly turns away from the conversation.

He focuses on getting a pen and a book from his bag, then spends the next two minutes staring at his arm with his back angled towards me.

Seth & Greyson

I spend the rest of class taking notes and mentally re-
playing my conversation with Seth, wondering what I said
that scared him off. When class ends, he hurries out the
door so quickly you'd think the room was on fire.

I try my best to stop stressing about what went wrong
with Seth and focus on school and meeting new people. I
have one of two photography classes today and end up
chatting with Jenna and Ari, a quirky couple who share my
same passion for photos. Jenna kind of reminds me of my
mom in the sense that she seems to teeter between reality
and dreamland.

"Oh, my God," she says as the three of us walk out of
class together. "You know what this means right?"

I exchange a look with Ari, who shrugs.

"We don't know what on earth your excitement could
possibly mean," he says, draping an arm around Jenna's
shoulder. "But please, do tell because we're dying to
know."

Her eyes light up with excitement as she tucks a stand
of purple hair behind her ear. "It means that my dream
came true, which means my wish of being psychic came
true."

"Dream?" I ask, intrigued. "Do tell me about this dream."

"It was about meeting you," she explains as we slowly move down the crammed hallway. "Before we started school here, I had a dream that we were going to meet someone who would become our friend."

"Jenna wants to be a psychic," Ari explains as he steers her toward the doors. "It's all she's talked about since she was twelve."

"You sound like my mother," I tell her as we push through the doors and step outside. "She's really into that stuff. And tarot cards."

"Oh, I love tarot cards," Jenna beams and Ari laughs, shaking his head. Clearly, he's heard this speech before. "You know what we should do tonight?"

"Study?" Ari suggests hopefully.

Jenna shakes her head and slams to a grinding halt right in the middle of a mob of students. "We should go downtown and check out Madame Sarine's Tarot Shop."

Ari scrunches his nose. "Do we have to? I'm kind of tired of getting my cards read."

"That's because you always get the death card."

"Which proves just how inaccurate tarot reading is."

She waves a finger and *tsks* him. "Don't insult the cards."

He tries to maintain his frown, but eventually heaves a sigh and surrenders. "Fine, I'll go, but only if Greyson comes, too." He looks at me pleadingly, as if he's crossing his fingers I'll reject the offer so he won't have to go himself.

"Sorry," I tell him. "But I really would like to get out of my apartment. I'm starting to go stir crazy."

Jenna claps her hands, jumping up and down and sticking her tongue out at Ari, who sighs again before chuckling.

"Fine, I'll go," he concedes. "But only if we can go home and get some work done before we go out."

Jenna agrees and we say our good-byes, the two of them waving as they head off toward the parking lot, leaving me to make the five-mile walk home by myself. I don't mind being alone, though. It gives me some time to clear my head.

My thoughts drift back over the day's events, feeling pretty content with the way it played out. Well, outside of

Seth freaking out on me. I can't stop stressing about what I could have possibly done wrong.

***

Before I go out with Ari and Jenna, I decide to pick up takeout because I'm tired of pizza. I call in my order before beginning the short walk to the restaurant, zipping up my jacket and pulling my hood over my head when the chilly evening air hits me. Staring up at the full moon, I think about what an awesome picture it would be and curse myself for not bringing my camera.

I'm almost to the restaurant when my phone rings. Fishing it out from my pocket, I smile when I see Jenna's name flash across the screen.

"What's up?" I answer, putting the phone up to my ear.

"Nothing," she says cheerfully. "We were just getting ready to head to your place, but then I realized I don't have your address."

"I'm actually walking right now to pick up some takeout."

"From which restaurant? We'll just meet you there."

Seth & Greyson

"I think it's called the Moonlight Diner." I glance up at the street sign as I approach the corner. "It's on Cherry and Peach."

"That sounds like the name of a slushy," she remarks.

"Oh! We should totally stop at the Snow Cone Palace on our way downtown."

I hear Ari holler something about being tired of snow cones and Jenna yells, "You can never get tired of snow cones." There's a pause and then she says, "Wait at the restaurant for us. We'll be there in ten."

"Okay. See you in a few." I hang up and pick up the pace, noting how much better I feel than I did just a few moments ago.

I don't know why I was so worried about making friends. I'm doing okay, at least with Ari and Jenna.

As I turn into the parking lot of the Moonlight Diner, though, I'm reminded that not all my friendly endeavors were a success.

Standing near the entrance doors below the neon signs and twinkling lights is Seth. He's near the ashtrays, smoking a cigarette and talking to a guy with short brown hair that I think is in my Biology class.

Seth is talking animatedly, his hands flailing through the air as he speaks. "I know. It's so crazy, right..." He trails off when he spots me.

Even though it's pretty dark, I can see him stiffen. He seems so uneasy about the prospect of talking to me that I consider letting him off the hook, but I'm fucking hungry and I'm not about to walk away from my dinner.

I cross the parking lot, stuffing my hands into my back pockets as I reach the two of them. "Hey, how's it going?"

"Oh, hey," Seth replies tensely. He glances at the guy then scratches his head and takes a drag of his cigarette. "What are you doing here?"

I point at the diner sign. "Getting takeout."

"Oh, right." He laughs nervously. "I almost forgot we were at a restaurant."

I don't know him very well, but his behavior seems strange and twitchy. Again, I wonder if I misread his signals earlier today when I thought he might be into me. But we held hands for so damn long and I know I saw him checking me out a time or two. Maybe he's nervous because he's still trying to find himself? Or perhaps he's on a date with this guy? I don't think the latter is the case, though. I'm not really picking up on a date vibe between them.

When a girl wearing a tight red dress comes strolling out of the restaurant, the guy Seth's with practically breaks his neck to check her out, cementing the fact that it's definitely not a date. So what's Seth's deal, then? Why go from friendly to standoffish in a snap of a finger?

When Seth notices me glancing back and forth between him and the guy, he lets out another nervous laugh. "Oh, yeah, introductions right?" He motions at the guy. "Luke, this is Greyson. Greyson, Luke."

I give Luke a small wave. "Yeah, I think we have bio together."

He nods, still somewhat distracted by the girl in the red dress. "It's nice to meet you, man."

An awkward silence settles between us, and I decide it's time to get my food before Jenna and Ari get here. I start for the door at the same time Seth steps for it and we slam into each other. I grab onto his arms as I start to stumble back and our gazes lock. His gaze drops to my lips and his fingers dig into my arms. A heartbeat goes by before he shuffles away from me, but it's enough time for me to see the want in his eyes beneath the overwhelming fear.

I realize Seth's afraid to be seen with me. While I was lucky to be born into an accepting family and never had too much of a problem openly being myself, I understand everyone isn't that lucky. Sadly, I'm guessing Seth is one of the unlucky ones.

I wish I could do something to help him. Hug him or something, tell him it's okay, that whatever happened to him is going to be fine. But unlike my mother, I don't believe I can see the future.

As I walk into the restaurant, I decide I'm going to make an effort to get to know him. If for nothing else than to be his friend.

Chapter 4

Seth

I hate how flustered and confused I feel after watching Greyson walk away from me. Part of me wants to apologize for my ridiculous behavior, but part of me is relieved. Luke doesn't seem like a judgmental person, but I can't seem to help my reaction. The same thing happened when we were holding hands in class earlier today and a football player took a seat in front of me, sending me straight into a flashback.

I know not every guy is Braiden, but I still find myself drowning in memories of my ex, the star quarterback at my high school and one hundred percent gorgeous. I never thought he'd be interested in me, but during a project we got paired up on, we ended up making out in my room. One hot and heavy make out session led to secret weekend hookups. Deep down, I think I always knew things would

47

end badly. Braiden wasn't openly gay and refused to see me outside the four walls of my garage. What I didn't expect was our relationship to end in such an ugly and brutal way.

I flinch at the memory and head back to the booth with Luke to join Callie and Kayden, who are engulfed in an intense conversation. While I'm curious about what they're discussing, my thoughts are still caught up in Greyson and the look on his face when he walked away.

He saw the fear inside me, the façade I put on that I'm always okay, always happy, all smiles, sunshine, and freakin' bedazzled unicorns.

On our way out of the restaurant, I contemplate talking to Callie about Greyson, but she's still pretty frustrated with me over inviting Kayden and Luke to dinner.

"I'm so going to get you back for this," she hisses under her breath as we head to the car.

"Why?" I whisper innocently. "I thought it went pretty well."

"It did, except for…" She bites her lip and looks down at her hands.

"Except for what?"

Seth & Greyson

"Except for when you left, Kayden tried to thank me and then he touched my hand." She wrings her hands in front of her with her head tipped down. "I freaked out and he probably thinks I'm even more of a weirdo then he did before."

Out of the corner of my eye, I sneak a peek at Kayden. His attention is focused solely on Callie, the worried look on his face proof of exactly how concerned he is about her.

"I really don't think that's what he's thinking," I tell her in a low voice.

She peers up at me. "Why not?"

Sliding my arm around her, I shoot her a grin rather than answer her question, realizing she's not ready to hear my predictions regarding the Callie/Kayden debacle. Sometimes you can just tell people belong together. Sometimes you just *know*.

Knowing is the easiest part. It's accepting and opening up that's complicated.

***

The weeks drift by in a sea of mind-numbing schoolwork. I spend a lot of my free time with Callie, and during class, I pretend not to notice Greyson. His hot-as-hell presence torments me, but I don't attempt to talk to him. I'm too mortified over my behavior at the restaurant and frustrated with myself for letting my past control me. Since life doesn't offer mulligans, I do the only thing I can. I just go with the flow.

I've just about convinced myself that I'm over my crush on Greyson when he leans toward me right in the middle of the professor's lecture. Just like that, I'm right back where I started. Completely obsessed.

"So, do you get anything he's saying?" he whispers under his breath.

My initial instinct is to look around and see if anyone is watching us, but I get caught up in the delicious scent of his cologne and blank out. "Yeah, a little bit."

His brow crooks. "You said you weren't a fan of school."

"Yeah, I'm not. It doesn't mean that I suck at all my classes, though. I just prefer not to have my head crammed with mostly useless knowledge."

His gaze drops to his open textbook then lands back at me. "Maybe you could tutor me, then. English isn't really my forte."

Seth & Greyson

I question whether he's being serious or just using tutoring as an excuse to hang out. "What is your forte? Because I'm really curious." My flirty tone comes out and shocks me a little.

"Photography." He pats his bag, where a camera strap is hanging out. "I actually got a scholarship. That's part of the reason why I ended up here."

The professor dismisses class and we start to gather our stuff.

"Seriously? That's fucking cool." I glance down at his bag as I stand to my feet and stretch out my arms. "Can I see some of your photos or is that too personal, like people with their journals?"

"No, it's okay." He gets to his feet, unzips his bag, and pulls out his camera.

"Are you sure? Sometimes I have issues with crossing the boundaries of personal space. Or so I've been told. Personally, I don't see it."

He chuckles as he taps a button, the screen lights up, and he hands it to me. "No, I promise you're cool. A lot of my photos have been entered in contests, so tons of people have seen them."

"Awesome." I hold the camera in my hands and try to figure out how to get to the slideshow.

He leans over, pressing a button on the screen, and his fingers brush mine before he pulls away. My stomach spins like a disco ball, but I focus on flipping through the photos.

Scrolling through each one, I notice a few landscapes, but most are of people. In each shot, he manages to capture a passionate sense of emotion. "Wow, these are amazing."

I'm a little stunned when I recognize the people in the next frame. I stop, staring down at a photo of me laughing with Callie outside on a bench. I tap to the next one and then the next, both of which are of me. In fact, the next twenty are all of me. Some I look happy in, but in a few, I see the pain I always carry with me.

I look over at Greyson. "When did you take these?"

With his brows furrowed, he leans over to see what I'm looking at. Then his eyes widen. "Fuck, I forgot those were on there." He snatches the camera away from me, shuts it off, and stuffs it into his bag. "I swear I'm not a stalker. I just saw you on the first day of school and," he slings his bag over his arm, and then fiddles with a leather bracelet on his wrist, "I don't know, I just wanted to take pictures of you."

Seth & Greyson

He's so embarrassed he's actually blushing, which is quite possibly the most adorable thing I've ever seen.

"It's okay," I tease, falling right back into the flirty again, for a moment being the old Seth. "I know how irresistible I can be."

A small smile rises on his lips as we head out of the classroom. "So, you're not completely weirded out?"

I shake my head. "Oddly, I'm kind of flattered, but that's probably the attention whore side of me speaking."

He peers around the empty room and then stares at me.

"What?" I pause in the doorway, suddenly feeling self-conscious.

"It's nothing. I just realized you never did answer me about the tutoring thing."

"You really need a tutor?" Because I'm highly suspicious that this is his way of asking me out.

"A little bit." The lie is written all over his face, but he doesn't seem like he's trying very hard to cover it up. "Maybe you could come over to my apartment tonight and help me with that stupid essay we're supposed to be writing. We could get some pizza or takeout."

As we step into the hallway, I open my mouth to answer, still unsure whether I'm going to reject or accept his offer. I never get to find out how brave I'm feeling today, because my phone goes nuts inside my pocket.

"Hold that thought." I hold up my finger while I dig out my phone from my pocket.

Callie: Hey, you want to go to a carnival tonight? Luke and I are headed to one.

Me: Luke and you? WTF?!?!? I thought you were into Kayden?

Callie: It's not like that. We're just friends. I helped him out with something today. And FYI, Kayden and I are just friends, too.

Me: Sure u r ;)

Callie: Le sigh.

Me: Don't le sigh me, baby girl.

Callie: So, will u come? It should be fun. Plus, I really need u there. I know Luke's cool and everything, but I still get nervous sometimes and Kayden's going to be there, too. I'll be the only girl.

Me: U know I'll always b there for u.

Callie: Thanks :) You're the best.

Me: Well, duh. That's kind of a given. I think I'll text Kayden and see if he wants a ride. I know he doesn't have a car.

Callie: Sounds good. Text me when u get there.

I send Kayden a text and we make plans to ride over together. Stuffing my phone back in my pocket, I offer Greyson an apologetic look as I squeeze past people crowding the hall. "Sorry, but I can't make it tonight." When his smile falters, I feel like the worst person in the entire universe. Well, besides Kayden's girlfriend, Daisy. That bitch is seriously evil. "I'd love to help you, but that was one of my friends on the phone. She needs my help with stuff," I stumble over my words as his frown deepens into a full-on pout. "Carnival stuff." As soon as I say it, I realize how stupid it sounded. "I swear to God, I'm not blowing you off. I just have this friend who has a hard time around guys and needs me to be there for her when she hangs out with the guy she likes."

"Is it that girl you were with in the photos?" he asks, relaxing a tad.

"Yeah, she's been through a lot and is always there for me. If it were anyone else, I would've said no. I promise."

"No, it's cool. I get it." He pauses, stopping near the exit doors. "I actually promised a couple of my friends I'd go to the carnival with them sometime this week, so maybe I'll head down tonight and we can meet up and hang out. Maybe ride the Ferris Wheel or something."

"Ferris Wheel?" I arch my brow at him. "Isn't that the one that takes forever to go around in a full circle? Like, the boringest ride ever?"

"What? I find it relaxing," he says with this sexy half-grin. "Besides, it's probably one of the best date rides ever because you get to spend all your time talking during the slow circle."

He waits for me to agree that we should meet up. I know what agreeing would mean, that I'm deciding to open myself up again, to love, to heartache, to pain.

My heart thrashes in my chest as I surprise myself and nod. "Okay, I'll see you there."

He grins as he takes out his phone. "What's your number? I'll text you when I get there."

I give him my phone number and he punches it into his contacts. Moments later, my phone vibrates from inside my pocket and I take it out.

Seth & Greyson

Unknown: Hey, it's Greyson. Thought you should have my number, too.

I fight back a grin, feeling stupidly happy, but I can't completely ignore the scars on my hand as I send him a reply text.

Chapter 5

Greyson

"Aw, man." Jenna sticks out her lip at the empty bag of cotton candy she's holding. "I'm tapped out."

We're at the carnival, wandering past the booths. The air smells like candy apples and funnel cakes, neon lights flash against the night sky, and dings and laughter flow around us.

"That's okay," Ari says, dragging his fingers through his long black hair. He's got on a leather jacket, even though it's seventy degrees out, and seems a little exhausted. "You've had so much already you have a sugar high."

Jenna shakes her head and her pout deepens. "I could eat at least two more bags."

"Fine, you can eat two more bags, but only if I get to stop on the way home and buy a six pack of energy drinks,"

Seth & Greyson

he challenges with his arms crossed and I wonder if keeping up with Jenna's nonstop energy caused his exhaustion.

Jenna crinkles her nose. "No way. You act like a yo-yo when you drink too many of those."

"A yo-yo?" I ask, laughing. "What does that even mean?"

She shoots Ari a conniving grin then says, "It means he's all over the place, like a crazy madman who can't sit still. Up and down and up and down. It drives me absolutely crazy."

"Well, I feel the exact same way when you eat too much sugar," he retorts with a smirk.

I laugh. The two of them have been going back and forth the entire night. I'm starting to realize it's their thing. They're really good together, though, and I find myself wishing I had someone to be that way with. With the guys I've dated in the past, I never felt connected enough.

"You look good tonight," Jenna says to me as she balls up the bag and chucks in into a nearby trash bin. "Do you have a hot date or something?" When I hesitate, her eyes light up. "You *so* do, don't you?"

59

"It's not a date," I clarify as we head toward the rides, pushing past a group of people who are either high on sugar or just really fucking happy to be at a carnival. "I just told someone I'd meet him here to hang out."

"Is it that guy you took all those pictures of?" she asks, slipping her fingers through Ari's.

I shrug, dodging around a couple making out in front of a balloon game. "Maybe."

Her lips curve to a grin. "I knew it." She trades a knowing look with Ari. "Didn't I tell you that the other day? That he was going to end up with the guy in all his pictures?"

Ari sighs a here-we-go-again sigh. "Yeah, you told me, but it doesn't mean you're a psychic."

"It *so* does, too." She sticks out her tongue then jerks on his arm. "Come on. You promised me you wouldn't be a baby this time and you'd ride the Zipper with me."

Ari's skin pales. "You know I hate super fast rides." He swallows hard as his gaze finds the spinning ride tucked in the far back corner. "And ones that go high."

"You promised me," she reminds him.

Seth & Greyson

He heaves a heavy sigh. "All right." He glances at me. "Greyson, you coming?"

Wanting to wait until Seth texts me, I shake my head. "I think I'm going to chill here for a while."

"And wait for the guy!" Jenna singsongs as she skips off toward the Zipper, towing a reluctant Ari behind her.

I lean against the side of a booth and watch people pass by to kill time. When ten minutes pass, I start to grow restless and wish I had my camera here. There's so many people around and with the crazy lighting going on, it'd make for some awesome pictures.

As more time passes, I turn to my camera phone and as discreetly as I can, sneak a picture of a guy and a girl making out on a booth kitty-corner from where I'm standing. I find it amazing to watch them, completely losing themselves in a sea of people, entirely oblivious to everything going on around them.

After I get the right shot, I put my phone away, starting to regret my decision to stay off the rides. While Seth and I didn't necessarily set a specific time to meet up, it's getting late. With how hot and cold he's been, I wouldn't be surprised if he stood me up.

As if he can read my doubtful thoughts, the phone suddenly vibrates. I dig it out and Seth's name flashes across the glowing screen.

Seth: Where r u?

I glance at the spinning ride beside me then message him back.

Me: By the Tilt-A-Whirl

Seth. A fast ride. Interesting. I thought you a take it slow, Ferris Wheel date kind of guy.

Me: Ha, ha. I never said I was solely a take it slow, Ferris Wheel kind of guy. I like fast rides, too.

"So, the Tilt-A-Whirl, huh?" Seth suddenly appears by my side.

He looks good in jeans and boots topped with a jacket over a button down shirt, making my grey thermal shirt and jeans that Jenna called my "dressed up look" seem plain and ordinary.

I blatantly check him out for a moment or two before I shove my phone into my pocket and skim the growing crowd. "Where's your friend? I thought you had to stay with her."

"Callie? She got on the Zipper with the guy she has a crush on." He considers something thoughtfully as he rolls his sleeves up. "She's starting to handle being around guys better than she thinks. I'm more of her security blanket than anything."

We start walking past the games and food booths, heading nowhere in particular.

"Can I ask why she's so afraid of guys?" I ask. "Or is that too personal?"

He wavers. "I can't get into the details, but I'll say it's because something really bad happened to her when she was young."

"Poor girl. You must really care about her, though. To take care of her like that."

"I feel like she's the sister I never had." He swings around the couple making out on the bench and then returns to my side. "Do you have any sisters?"

I shake my head. "I'm an only child."

"Me, too." He frowns, appearing unhappy about this. "Doesn't it suck, having all the attention on you twenty-four seven?"

I shrug, kicking at the dirt. "I really don't mind it. My parents are actually pretty cool, albeit a little weird and eccentric."

He angles his head to the side. "What do you mean by weird and eccentric?"

"Well, my mom is a nonpracticing psychic/tarot card reader whose hobbies include making pot brownies on the weekend for her yoga club. And my father is an herbalist who spends a lot of time with my mom, her pot brownies, and the yoga club."

He snorts a laugh, his eyes crinkling around the corners. "They actually sound pretty fun. I bet you had a blast growing up."

"It was definitely interesting. I mean, I had access to pot brownies and can even make them myself. I know how to cleanse my aura and what herbs are best to take when you're sick. But I don't know," I pause, stuffing my hands into my back pockets. "Sometimes it felt like I was more of the parent than the child."

He stares at the sky, looking as if he's contemplating his next words. When he meets my gaze again, he seems nervous. "Does she... Do your parents know that you're..."

"That I'm gay?" I finish for him.

Relief washes over his face as he nods. "Yeah."

"Yeah, I told them when I was fourteen. It was one of the hardest things I've ever had to do." Stepping around a bench, I make a left toward a ticket booth. "What about you?

"My mom knows," he says tightly, staring out at the quiet street next to the fairgrounds.

"What about your dad?" I ask as I dig my wallet out of my pocket.

"He's been out of the picture for a while."

"Fuck. Sorry, man." I feel like an ass for bringing it up.

He shrugs me off. "It's fine. He was kind of an ass-hole, anyway, so I really don't care."

I pull a ten out of my wallet and slide it through the hole at the bottom of the ticket window. "So, your mom. How did she react?"

He scratches his cheek, seeming uneasy. "She's a very old-fashioned woman so…" He shrugs.

I want to smack myself on the head for opening my mouth. "Fuck, I'm sorry I brought it up."

"You don't have to keep apologizing. You didn't know. And besides, that's in the past. I've moved on…" He glances down at his arm and a pucker forms at his brow. "Sort of." He blows out a breath then smiles up at me, going from night to day in the snap of a finger. "But anyway, let's talk about something else." His gaze glides toward the booths. "Like why the hell a girl wearing a poodle skirt is flailing her arms at us."

I collect the tickets from the cashier, put my wallet back into my pocket, and then track his gaze, finding Jenna waving her hands at us with a grin plastered on her face. "Oh, that's Jenna."

"The friend you came here with?" he asks and I nod. "She seems… super happy." His head tilts to the side as he muses over something before a slow grin spreads across his face. "I think I like her already."

Jenna comes racing over and without warning, throws her arms around Seth. "Oh, my God! It's so nice to finally meet Hot Picture Guy."

Seth cocks a brow at me from over her shoulder and mouths, *Hot Picture Guy?* Then he laughs when I get a little uncomfortable.

Seth & Greyson

I was so fucking embarrassed when he saw those pictures on my camera and it still makes me feel uncomfortable, even if Seth seemed more flattered than creeped out.

Seth gives Jenna this huge hug back and even bounces up and down with her.

"I love, love your outfit," he says when they pull back. "It's very fifties retro."

Jenna fiddles with the hem of her skirt. "Thanks. I love shopping at vintage stores. You can find so much amazing stuff there."

"You like to shop?" Seth asks excitedly.

"Duh. Totally."

"Me, too. Maybe I'll go with you sometime."

Jenna glances at me, as if asking for my permission.

I wave her off. "I don't care. You can do whatever you want."

She claps her hands and squeals. "Awesome." She starts backing away. "I'm going to go check up on Ari. I just wanted to see how things were going."

"Where is Ari?" I ask her, searching the mob of people for him.

"Oh, he threw up," she tells me solemnly. "He couldn't handle the ride."

She whirls on her heels and hurries off toward the bathroom stalls across from us.

"She's fun," Seth comments as he turns to me.

"Yeah, she'll definitely keep you on your toes." With the tickets in my hand, I nod my head in the direction of the Ferris Wheel and motion for Seth to follow. "I only met her a few weeks ago, but she and her boyfriend have been pretty cool. They've made starting over easy, too."

"Why did you decide to leave Florida?" he asks. As we pass by a large group of guys around our age, he seems to grow really nervous and puts at least ten feet between us.

His edginess seems to amplify when one of the guys turns and looks in our direction. Seth looks like he's one step away from panicking. I want to reach out and take his hand, tell him to relax, but I worry that will only make him freak out more.

Seth & Greyson

"I mean, I know you got a scholarship, but that's still a pretty big move just for school," he continues on after the guys have disappeared from our sight.

I try not to be bothered by his move, but it stings a little. "My parents didn't have a whole lot saved up, so that was part of the reason." I massage the back of my neck as I get in line. "I don't know, though. I also sort of wanted to start over and make decisions for myself. My parents are cool, but they rely on me a lot. Plus, I got a rep for being..." I trail off before I make myself look like a douchebag.

"Rep for what?" Seth inquires, clearly intrigued.

I consider sugarcoating it, but I've never been that great a liar. "It's going to make me come off as a douche, so promise you won't judge me."

"Trust me, I would never judge you."

"Okay, well, I got a rep for being a closed-off manwhore." I move forward with the line. "It's not true. Well, not really. I'm just..."

"Shy?" he tries. "Because it doesn't seem that way. At all, really."

"No, it's not that." I pause, staring up at the ride as it twirls the carts toward the night sky. "Sometimes, I get the feeling that I come off as an out of place, awkward loner, if that makes sense."

"That makes perfect sense." He steps forward as the line moves. "So, were you one of those angsty teenagers who wrote tortured poetry?"

I chuckle as I elevate my brows. "The fifteen year old version of me was kind of like that, but I outgrew that phase by the time I was sixteen. That was mainly because my mother took away all of my music, my computer, even my camera and threatened to never give it back unless I got out of the house more and lived a little."

"Even though you might hate me for saying this, I think your mother sounds fabulous."

"She can be, in her own way. But living with her can get intense."

We shuffle forward with the line and finally reach the ramp. I hand the carnie six tickets then we hop into the seat and he locks the bar. With a jerk, the wheel spins, taking us upward. Eighties rock blasts from the stereo and fills up the silence between us.

Seth & Greyson

Seth grips the bar, frowning at the ground. "I'm not a fan of heights."

Feeling daring, I slide my fingers along the bar and place my hand over his. His skin is warm beneath mine and I trace circles on it with my thumb, getting completely turned on. Fuck, it's been awhile. In fact, it's been too long. "I promise I won't let anything happen to you." I glance at his lips and think about kissing him right there on the slow ass Ferris Wheel, maybe even touching him a little.

He stares at our interlocked fingers then tensely looks around at the young couple in the cart above us and at the giggle girls in the cart below us before moving our hands down to the seat between us. He's worried someone will see us, and again, I don't have a fucking clue how to react. All my life, I've been taught to be proud of who I am. With the exception of a few angsty teenage years I spent searching for myself, I've done just that. Yes, I had moments where I was terrified out of my damn mind. The first time I held hands with another guy in public. During my first kiss. When I told my parents I was gay, I was shaking so badly I could hardly breathe, but with time, I started feeling like I was settling into who I am.

He offers me a nervous smile. "Sorry."

"It's okay," I say, but I don't think I really mean it.

"Okay, so, I have to ask," he says, changing the subject. "Where'd the manwhore rep come from?"

I pull a face. "That wasn't my fault."

"Oh, yeah?" His brow arches skeptically. "Cause that kind of sounds like a line."

"I swear it's not, though. There's a huge, long story behind it."

When the cart rocks, Seth's grip tightens on my hand. "Do tell, please."

I sigh. "You're not going to let this go, are you?"

He shakes his head. "The first thing you should know about me is I never let anything go that intrigues me."

"Fine. I'll give you the short version... When I first started dating, I dated a lot, but mainly because I had such a hard time talking to guys. Every time I went out, I would freeze up and things would get really awkward."

"You keep saying how awkward you were and how hard it was for you to talk to people, but it doesn't make sense to me. You seem okay now."

"I'm getting better," I say with a shrug. "Plus, you're easy to talk to."

Grinning, he points a finger at me. "That is definitely true."

"Sometimes I have a hard time figuring out what to say, though, and I end up staring at the person in silence, which makes me come off as either angry or just plain weird."

We laugh as the cart reaches the bottom and starts to round toward the top again.

"Okay, so now you have to tell me some stuff about you," I say, relaxing back in the seat.

Seth's mouth sinks to a frown. "There's really not much to tell."

"I doubt that."

"Okay, you're right, but my story is…" His gaze falls to his arm again.

That's when I notice the faint scars crisscrossing his arm, hand, and fingers.

"What happened?" I reach out with my free hand, tracing my fingertip across one of the longer scars marring his forearm.

He shivers from my touch, but quickly pulls away and tucks his arm to his side. "It's a long story."

I press my lips together to stop myself from pressing him for details. It's clearly a touchy subject for him, and I have to wonder if his scars have anything to do with why he's so skittish about PDA.

"Hold on a second." He retrieves his phone from his pocket and then frowns at the screen. "Shit. I have to go meet up with Callie."

I can't tell if he's lying, but from my angle, it looks like he's staring at a blank screen.

"That's cool. Want to catch up later?"

"Maybe." He puts his phone away then turns to me. "But only if you promise we can ride something that moves faster than a snail."

"All right. I'm down," I say, grinning.

We hold hands and talk a bit more as we make the final loop, but Seth quickly pulls away as the carnie approaches us and lets us out. He waves goodbye and I head off to find Jenna and Ari.

I spend the rest of the night hanging out with the two of them and texting Seth. Around midnight, he says he's sorry, but he won't be able to meet up tonight, that Callie needs him. I'm a bit confused whether he's being truthful or running away again. Still, by the end of the night, I've texted him so much that it might be a record for me. All the conversations seem to focus on me, though, and I find myself wishing I knew him better. Maybe then I could understand what's going on in his head. Starting with what the fuck put those scars on his arm.

Chapter 6

Seth

I feel like the most tragic person that's ever existed. Not only did I act like a spaz when Greyson tried to hold my hand, but then I blew him off. It wasn't entirely my fault, though. I was planning on meeting up with him later like I said, but then something happened between Kayden and Callie while they were on the playground ride at the carnival. Whatever went down has her looking alternately high as a kite and sullen as a Goth girl.

"So, do you want to share what that weird look on your face is about?" I ask after we make it back to my dorm room.

Callie is spending the night, something she's been do-ing a lot lately because her skank-of-a-roommate made a rule that Callie couldn't enter when a red scarf was hanging on the doorknob. The damn thing practically hangs on the door twenty-four seven, so much that I wonder how the girl can even walk.

Callie remains quiet as I kick off my boots and climb into my unmade bed.

Then she lies down next to me and rests her cheek on the pillow. "You really want to know?"

"Heck, yeah. You look like you're high." I roll to my side and prop up on my elbow. "Wait a minute. Is that what you were doing up there? Were you getting high?"

She swats my arm. "No... we were... kissing."

The look of fear in her eyes causes me to laugh. "You say that like it's so wrong."

She shrugs, staring at her hands. "It feels like it should be wrong... the last time someone kissed me, that's how it felt."

I sigh. "That's because the last time it *was*. But not this time. This time it was right. Both of you wanted it. Right?"

She bites back a smile. "It was a really nice kiss."

For a brief moment, I feel jealous of her. It's been so long since I've been kissed and after what happened, the memories of those kisses feel tainted. With the way Greyson was looking at me tonight, I knew if I went in for the kiss, he would have kissed me back. But once again, I've become a walking tragedy and let my past control me.

Knowing I need to be happy for Callie, though, I jump up and bounce on the mattress. "Okay, tell me how it went. What were you doing? And how did it happen?"

She sits up and reclines against the headboard. "He said that whole challenge thing was a setup to get me up there."

I roll my eyes. When Kayden told us about that lame challenge of seeing who could get through the playground ride first, I knew it was a setup. "Well, duh. I got that they were up to something."

"Really." She frowns. "I thought they were just being guys."

"Oh, they were," I assure her. "Relax, it was all for fun and he got to kiss you just like he was trying to do the whole night."

She hugs a pillow to her chest. "Yeah, but did he seem a little offish when we left?"

"He seemed tired, but not offish."

Seth & Greyson

She fastens her hair into a messy bun. "So, what was that thing with that guy you were talking about?"

My pulse quickens just thinking about Greyson. How easy it was to talk to him. How amazing it felt when he touched my hand. Even though I acted like a weirdo toward the end, it was still a great night.

"We hung out for a while on the Ferris Wheel." I take out my phone. "I got his phone number earlier and we were texting for like half the night. It was pretty amazing."

"I'm so happy for you. Are you going to go out with him?"

"Maybe." Deciding not to dwell on the negative, I relax in the bed and smile. "God, it was such a great night."

She stares up at the ceiling with a content look on her face. "It really was."

A few minutes later, I doze off dreaming of Ferris Wheels, soft circles, and the way Greyson kept staring at my lips.

Eventually the dream shifts, though. I'm no longer at the carnival, but on the ground. Feet and fists are slamming against my side as people shout hateful words at me. They don't even know me; they hate me simply because I'm different. So much hate pollutes the air that I can barely breathe. I use my arm to protect my head from the blows and feel the bones snap as someone stomps on it.

As blinding pain shoots through my body, I blink up through the blood and dirt and see a familiar face looking down at me, only it can't be right. Braiden never looks at me like that, like he hates me so much he can't stand it.

The look hurts more than the fists and the kicks.

Chapter 7

Seth

The next day I wake up with a pounding headache and an overwhelming urge to skip out on class, so I do. I spend the morning going through my clothes and putting outfits together, working on my homework, and avoiding Greyson's texts. Deep down, I know he's not Braiden. He's already proven that by simply being seen in public with me, but the nightmares make the wounds on my arm feel too fresh.

Around eleven, I'm waiting outside of Callie's dorm room while she gets dressed so we can go get some breakfast. My phone buzzes from inside my pocket and I tense as I open the message.

Greyson: Hey, haven't heard from u. Hope everything is okay with Callie. Anyway, call me when you get a chance. Jenna's making me go to this art show next

Friday and she suggested I bring u too so we can double date.

As soon as I finish reading the message, another text buzzes through.

Greyson: Okay, so I totally just reread my message and realized how lame a double date probably sounds. I promise, though, it'll be fun. There's free wine and food and we can leave the moment it gets boring.

My finger hovers over the buttons as I deliberate how to reply. He's asking me out on a date. Like a real date *date*.

"Hey, man." Luke strolls up to me, zipping up his jacket. "I was actually heading to your dorm."

"Why?" I ask, shoving my phone away without replying.

"I actually need a favor."

"Are we to the favor stage yet?" I joke as I tame my hair with my fingers.

He chuckles then bobs his head from side to side. "I was kind of hoping we were."

"Okay." I wait for him to explain.

He huffs out a breath. "I need to borrow your car."

My brows knit. "Where's your truck?"

"Kayden borrowed it so he could drive home for prom." His jaw tightens in annoyance.

"Prom?" I frown. "What the hell?"

He lifts his shoulder and shrugs. "His girlfriend back home is a senior and he promised her he'd take her."

My lip instinctively curls. "Seriously? He's still dating that Barbie bitch I met a couple weeks ago?"

Luke barks a laugh. "I really like that description of her."

I don't find it funny at all. "I thought Kayden broke up with her." I glance over my shoulder at Callie's door, hoping she can't hear.

"He did, but he promised Daisy he'd go with her before they broke up," he says with another shrug. "Honestly, I don't get it, but for some reason, Kayden can't seem to just tell her no. He's always been that way, though."

Suddenly, the door behind me swings open, and Callie walks out, slipping on a hoodie. I try to keep a lock on my expression, but my smile falters when she grins at me.

She immediately stiffens. "What's wrong?"

Luke has a guilty look on his face as he waves at her. "Hey, Callie, what's up?"

She self-consciously combs her hands through her hair. "Nothing much. Seth and I are just headed out to get some breakfast."

"Yeah, we were just talking about that." Luke backs down the hall, totally bailing out on the situation. "I was asking Seth if I could borrow his car, but I'll just find someone else."

I glare at him for leaving me to break the news to her, and he quickens his pace.

"Why? Where's your truck?" Callie calls out.

"Kayden took it somewhere." He waves at us, then spins on his heels and jogs down the hallway like a coward. "I'll catch up with you two later," he calls over his shoulder.

Callie's eyes swarm with confusion. "What was that all about?"

I hook my arm through hers, deciding just to rip the band-aid off. "We need to talk."

Seth & Greyson

We push out the doors at the end of the hallway and step outside beneath the grey sky. Dry leaves gust across the grass and the trees move with the wind.

"Are you going to tell me why you're looking at me like you're about to tell me my dog died?" she asks as we head for the parking lot.

I drag out the silence for as long as possible, rummaging to get my keys out. "I have something to tell you and I don't know how you're going to take it." I let go of her arm, unlock the doors, and get in.

I start the engine, crank up the heat, then scroll through my playlists on my iPod. "Kayden borrowed Luke's truck." I set the iPod down and internally cringe as I say, "To go back home for a few days... to go to prom."

She buckles her seatbelt. "Okay, why are you acting weird?"

I shove the shifter into reverse and glance over my shoulder as I back out of the parking spot. "Well, because he didn't say anything to you. Wait a minute. Did he tell you?"

She shakes her head. "No, but why would he? We barely know each other."

I don't like her reaction at all. It shows how little self-esteem she has, and makes me hate the guy that hurt her even more. It also makes me kind of hate Kayden for adding to her pain. "Callie, you made out with him last night and let him feel your boob."

"Hey," she protests, crossing her arms over her chest. "I told you that in confidence."

I steer the car onto the road. "Relax, I'm just pointing out how big a step that was for you. An important step. You wouldn't just do it with any guy."

"I like Kayden, but it doesn't mean he has to tell me everything he does. I'm not his girlfriend. "

"So what." I turn down the stereo volume. "He should have said something instead of just taking off. He knew you'd probably want to see him. And you know his darkest secret, Callie, which is the hardest part about getting to know someone."

I glance down at the scars on my arm and think about the secrets connected to them. The only person I've ever told was Callie and my mother. My mother refused to acknowledge anything happened. She wouldn't let me report the assault, said no one would care. In a way, I hate her for it, for not being there for me when I needed her, for making me feel so ashamed.

Chapter 8

Seth

I'm still avoiding Greyson to the point that I cut out on English class again. I never replied to his offer of going to see the art show next Friday and haven't heard anything from him since. I'm starting to think he's given up on me and even convince myself I'm grateful. Clearly, I'm not ready for another relationship yet.

But if that's true, why do I feel like a walking depressant all the time? I want to be my sparkling self again, the one who runs wild, laughs all the damn time, and feels comfortable in his own skin. I'm seriously one step away from going all emo, locking myself in my room, and putting the dreariest song I can find on repeat.

Thankfully, I have Callie and her problems to keep me preoccupied from doing so.

Seth & Greyson

"Why do you keep making air quotes?" she asks me during class.

Even though she's been reluctant to talk about how she's feeling, I've keep pushing her to open up. I can tell she's upset about the Daisy thing even though she won't admit it.

I lean over in the desk and whisper. "Because I'm quoting what it said in my psych book?"

"Your psych book talked about my problem?" she asks, unzipping her bag.

"Not specifically, but it was close." I chew on the end of the pen as I sit up straight in my chair.

She drops her books into her bag and I jot down a few notes before class lets out. We wait until the room has cleared before we head down the stairs.

Professor Jennerly, a gangly man who likes to wear sport coats with elbow patches and eighties style glasses, is waiting by the door when we walk out.

"My classroom is not for outside chit chat," he scolds. "If you two want to talk, then I suggest you stay out of my class."

"We're sorry." I glance at Callie and roll my eyes. "It'll never happen again."

He scowls at us as we exit the room. "It better not."

I roll my eyes again. "What a drama queen."

Callie giggles. "Well, we were talking through half his class."

"That's because it's either talk or fall asleep." I force a yawn then loop my arm through hers. "That class is seriously so boring.

She laughs again as we head down the hallway toward the exit doors. She starts staring out the window at the domed football stadium in the distance, the one where most of Kayden's games are played.

"Are you thinking about him?" I ask, nudging her in the side.

She rips her attention away from the stadium and focuses on me. "Thinking about who?"

I shake my head. "Callie, you need to either forget about him or talk to him. You can't just keep avoiding him, yet wanting him."

Seth & Greyson

"I don't want him," she lies. When I frown, she sighs. "Alright, fine. Yes, I think about him. A lot. But I'll get over him. God, I barely know him."

"Yet you two shared a lot," I flatten my palm to the door and push it open. "You saved him. He was the first guy you ever trusted. He gave you your first real kiss."

"I trusted you first." She digs through her purse, pulling out a pack of gum.

"That's not the same." I hold the door and we step outside. "I'm a friend. Kayden was more than a friend."

"I don't know if that's true." She pops a piece of gum into her mouth and offers me one. "I don't know what I feel for him or if it was good or bad. In fact, sometimes I still feel like that scared little girl who doesn't know what to do with anything."

I take a piece of gum, unwrapping it before chewing thoughtfully. "Well, maybe you should do whatever the hell you want instead of what you think you should do." I pause as soon as I say it, processing the full meaning of my words.

Callie isn't the only one who could benefit from the advice I've been giving her the last few weeks. I've been lecturing her over and over about coming out of her shell and going after what she wants. I've urged her countless times to stop allowing her past and her fear to control her, but here I am doing the same Goddamn thing with Greyson.

Fuck me. Why have I been so blind?

The question is, what am I going to do about it? Continue hiding or stop being so damn scared?

She aims a finger at me accusingly. "You just quoted that from the list."

I let out an evil laugh, throwing my head back. "That's because it's quote day. Didn't you get the memo?"

A laugh escapes her lips. "Darn it. I forgot to check my messages today. I must've missed it."

I swing an arm around her shoulder and pull her close. "The question is, what do you want to do? And I mean really, really want?"

I know what I want. I really, really do. I just need to find the courage to go after it.

She stops near a bench and gazes at the stadium. "I want to have fun."

Seth & Greyson

"Now fun is definitely something I can help you with." I thrum my finger against my lip. "I just need to know how big you want to go."

She considers my request. "I want to go big. Because it's either go big or go home, right? And the last thing I want to do is go home."

"Me, too." A mischievous smile spreads across my face. "All right, my Callie girl. Let's go have some fun."

***

Five hours later, the sun has set, the night has come alive, and Callie and I are smack dab in the middle of it. It's been a long time since I've gotten out and had some good old drunken fun and with five drinks in me, I'm feeling pretty good. So good, in fact, that I'm okay with being at the frat party where we've somehow ended up. Callie and I are dancing and letting our hair down, partying like rockstars.

"I'm so glad we decided to do this!" Callie shouts over the music, fanning her hand in front of her face.

I glance at the people around the room, dancing, laughing, drinking, all in their own little worlds. "Me, too!"

She giggles and I giggle.

"I really have no clue what's so funny," I say through my laughter. "But God, it feels so good to laugh!"

I let the music take over and really get into it, but slow down the energy when I spot Greyson in the corner with that girl Jenna and her boyfriend. Greyson is drinking from a plastic cup and the three of them are laughing at something. I wonder if he knows I'm here and if so, why he hasn't come over and said hello. Then I remember what an asshole I've been lately. Even if he realizes I'm here, I wouldn't blame him for not approaching me.

Tearing my attention away from Greyson and his friends, I search the room for the alcohol, but end up stumbling across something way more interesting than vodka. Luke and Kayden are standing by the front door with two girls, neither of whom are Daisy. Goddamn him. I seriously want to hurt him right now for doing this to Callie.

"Whatcha lookin' at?" Callie asks with a slight slur to her speech.

I glance down at her big, glossed-over eyes, deciding it might be time to cut her off. "Nothing." When she starts to glance towards the door, I grab her by the shoulders. "Okay, it's not nothing." I sigh. "Kayden's here… and he's not alone."

Seth & Greyson

Her eyes widen. "He's with a girl?"

"Yeah… maybe we should just go. You can walk out of here with your head held high and pretty much tell him to go fuck himself. Wouldn't that be fun?"

She smashes her lips together, shakes her head, and turns around. "I want to talk to him," she mutters before stumbling through the crowd toward Kayden.

She weaves around people and I follow her, trying to gauge Kayden's reaction. He seems surprised to see her and, oddly, kind of relieved. I cross my fingers and toes that both girls are with Luke and Kayden came here in hopes of running into Callie.

Please, please, don't let him be a douchebag.

When Callie reaches him, she flings her arms around his neck. "Kayden's here," she says, hugging him like he's a giant teddy bear.

He puts his hand on her back, a protective gesture that calms me down a bit. "Are you drunk?"

She pulls back, bobbing her head up and down. "A little."

"No, she's wasted." I roll up the sleeves of my jacket and wipe the sweat from my forehead. "And I mean fucking trashed."

Callie rests her head on Kayden's chest and he stiffens. "I thought she didn't drink that much?" he asks me.

I shrug, my focus wandering to the corner of the room. Greyson is still there and a group has formed around him, something I find deeply amusing. He says he's so awkward, yet people obviously like and gravitate toward him. I really don't get his reservations about his personality. Even I felt comfortable around him. Well, as comfortable as can be expected around someone who makes my heart race and my palms sweat. I want to go tease him about it, and I think I might have just enough alcohol in my system to do so.

"She doesn't, but tonight she did." I glance back at Kayden. "Look, can you watch her for just a little bit? There's someone I need to talk to."

He nods, tracing his fingers down her spine. "Sure," he says, so absorbed with Callie that he doesn't even glance in my direction.

He almost looks like a lovesick puppy. Granted, a terrified-out-of-his-mind lovesick puppy. That doesn't mean I fully trust him, though. He has a lot of wrongs to right if he's going to prove he's good enough to deserve my Callie.

"And make sure to keep your hands to yourself," I back away with my finger pointed at him. "She's drunk enough that she won't remember a thing, which makes any touching on your part wrong."

His jaw drops somewhere near his knees. "What kind of guy do you think I am?"

I stare at him pointedly, raising an eyebrow. "I have no idea."

I turn on my heel and push my way through the crowd and over to Greyson. His eyes widen when he sees me coming.

"Hey, what're you doing here?" he asks, gripping the cup in his hand.

With my gaze fixed on him, I try to ignore the people around us and hitch my thumb over my shoulder in Callie's direction. "Callie wanted to have fun, so I took her out and got her drunk."

His eyes light up as he laughs. "So that's your idea of fun."

I bob my head from side to side, considering. "One of many, I guess."

He glances at Jenna, who gives him a knowing look and offers me a wave.

"Hey, Seth. How's it going?" In her sparkling silver dress with diamonds in her hair, she looks like a bag of glitter threw up on her.

"Good. I've been meaning to call you so we could go shopping."

"I totally should've called you the other day when I was out, but..." She trails off when Greyson gives her a pressing look. "You know what, I think I'm going to go get a drink." She snags Ari's arm and tugs him off toward the kitchen area.

I look at Greyson. "Did I say something wrong?"

He shakes his head, looking uneasy, and raises the cup to his lips to finish off the drink. I use the opportunity to check him out. He's wearing a black shirt with a red logo on it, his jeans are the perfect fit—not too tight or too lose—and his hair has a sexy bedhead look to it.

He lowers the cup, crunches it in his hand, and chucks it into a nearby trashcan. When he locks his eyes on me again, I know what's coming and prepare myself for the impact.

"So, I haven't seen or heard from you pretty much since the carnival." He stuffs his hands into the back pockets of his jeans and rocks back on his heels. "At first I thought maybe it was because you were avoiding me, but then I realized how self-centered believing you'd actually cut class over me seemed." He studies me closely and I try not to get all wiggly. "Is everything okay?"

I don't know how to respond to him. My first thought is to feed him some hyped up, overdramatic excuse because I'm good at giving those. But then I remember my revelation in the campus yard about how I need to start taking my own advice.

"Actually, I *was* avoiding you," I shamefully admit.

His lips part in shock. "Wow, I didn't expect you to be so honest."

"Usually, I'm an honest person. Too honest sometimes. But I get where you're coming from. I haven't really been myself around you. Not completely, anyway."

He swallows hard. "Is it something I've done or said? Because I know I can get a little weird—"

"No, it's not you at all," I cut him off, feeling like the biggest asshole. "It's me." He looks befuddled, so I add, "Some stuff happened to me in my past that makes me..." The scars on my hand throb. I feel so vulnerable standing there in front of him, trying to explain the secret I've kept locked inside me. "Hesitate."

His gaze flicks to the scars on my arm. "Do you want to talk about it?"

"Maybe in the future." Once I say it, I realize how much I mean it. One day, I hope I can tell him what happened without being terrified out of my mind. "But tonight was supposed to be about fun."

"So, you want to have fun, then?" he asks with a dare in his eyes.

I feel like I might be getting in over my head, but I'm too drunk to back down. "That all depends. What did you have in mind?"

Lust fills his eyes and the look instantly fills my thoughts with lots and lots of dirty images of the fun things we could do. He stands up straight and motions for me to follow him through the dancing crowd. I trail at his heels and note every single person that so much as glances in our direction, wondering what they're thinking or if they're thinking anything. I really wish my mind was calm, but it's racing a zillion miles a minute.

My adrenaline goes up a thousand notches when Greyson makes a right and turns down a hallway lined with a few open doors, all of which lead to bedrooms. I start to get so turned on just thinking about going in one of them. But the last time I was with someone intimately was with Braiden. Since I can't even talk about what happened yet, I don't think I'm ready to go down that road, despite how much my body wants to.

I open my mouth to tell Greyson I need to leave, but close my trap when he enters a room with a heavy game of poker going on.

"You're into cards?" I question, staring at the table covered with poker chips and cards.

"It's okay. It can be really fun when you're drunk."

"Are you drunk?"

"Are you?"

I mentally try to calculate a problem using the quadratic formula I learned in Pre-Cal, but then realize I couldn't even figure out the answer sober.

"What are you thinking about?" Greyson's gaze zeros in on my lips and desire fills his eyes.

"You really want to know?" I ask and he nods. "The quadratic formula."

The desire deflates like a balloon. "What?"

"Never mind." I nod at the table five guys and three girls are seated around. "So, are we going to play?"

"Do you know how?"

"Of course."

A thoughtful look crosses his face. "Okay, good, because I want to make a wager."

"A wager?"

"Yeah, if I win more than you, you have to go to this art show with me."

I hesitate. "And if I win?"

He shrugs. "You can have anything you want."

My skin warms as thousands of very vivid images of what I want flash through my mind.

"All right, you have a deal." I stick out my hand to shake on it.

Seth & Greyson

He wraps his hand around mine, grips tightly and slides his finger along the inside of my wrist as he pulls away.

"Can I just say again that I seriously don't understand why you think you're awkward," I tell him. "You're kind of the exact opposite."

"Well, I'm kind of a little drunk right now, so the alcohol puts the weirdo inside me to sleep."

I shake my head, laughing under my breath. "Okay, let's get this over with."

"Wait, aren't you going to tell me what you want if you win?" he asks, rolling his tongue along the inside of his mouth to stop himself from grinning.

I shake my head. "Nope. You're just going to have to wait until after I win."

His eyes glimmer with amusement as I hedge around him and take a seat at the table. He sits down beside me, we both buy a fair amount of chips, and the game begins. We're not really playing against everyone else, so Greyson and I keep our own little tally as hand after hand is dealt. I'm a pretty decent player, but Greyson seems to be a bit better. He keeps smirking in my direction, like he's sure he's going to kick my ass.

Two hours later, I've gotten lost in the game and the worry about everyone watching me has dissipated. The downside, I've lost all my chips and the wager we made. My stomach churns as we leave the table and the party, knowing that I have no excuse not to go with him to the art show. Whether I'm over my fear or not, I have to go out on a date with him.

"A penny for your thoughts?" he asks as we stroll up the sidewalk toward the campus that's a few blocks away.

"I was just thinking about how much I hate to lose." I fake a pout. "I'm an extremely sore loser."

"And I'm kind of an arrogant winner." He forces a smirk, but then busts up laughing. "Okay, actually I'm not. In fact, I kind of feel bad that you lost."

"Enough to let me win, perhaps?"

"No way. I'm holding you to our deal. Besides, I hate going to these art shows by myself. The room is always so stuffy and so are most of the people."

"But you're an art major."

"Yeah, but it doesn't mean I fit the mold of art gallery people."

We pause at the corner, checking for traffic before stepping off the curb to cross the street. My head is still spinning a bit, and I'm not sure if it's the alcohol or Greyson. The streets are mostly deserted at this hour and it's so quiet I can almost pretend that Greyson and I are the only two people who exist. If only I could feel that way all the time. Life would be so much easier.

"I'll tell you what." Greyson walks backwards so he's facing me. "How about we consider both of us winners? You go to the art show with me and you get one thing of your choice."

"You know, you're putting a lot of trust in me right now," I say as I hop up onto the sidewalk. "Giving me free reign to do whatever I want, especially when I have such a wild imagination."

He stops walking and I almost run into him. "Okay, now you've got me wondering what the hell you're going to pick."

I flash him a wicked smirk. "Oh, no. I'm not going to pick something right away. I'm going to wait until the perfect moment and spring it on you."

He restrains a grin as we start walking again. "Fine. But you still have to go to the art show with me. That's the deal."

I nod, shaking, terrified to death. "It's next Friday night, right?"

He nods, slowing down as we reach the front of my lofty dorm building. Most of the lights are off and the air carries a stillness to it.

"So, this is me," I tell him, digging my keycard out of my pocket.

I'm not sure what exactly I'm supposed to do. Invite him in? Yeah, I'm sure my roommate would love that. Then again, he's never there.

I press my hand to my head. God, I'm getting a headache from the stress.

"I need to get home," Greyson says, and if I didn't know any better, I'd guess he was saving me from my inner conflict. "But I'll call you tomorrow and give you all the details about the show. The time, place, and whatnot. Jenna and Ari are going to be driving. I hope that's okay."

"Of course." I turn to slide the keycard through the slot, feeling flustered for some reason.

106

Seth & Greyson

"Seth," he says tentatively as I'm opening the door.

I pause without turning around. "Yeah." My voice shakes a little, which is ridiculous.

I've never been the nervous type, not even the first time Braiden and I kissed. It just kind of happened and I felt excited, but never nervous.

His hand touches my arm and he gives me a little tug. I turn around without thinking and he leans in and brushes his lips against mine. He kisses more tentatively than I'm used to, as if he's nervous, too, which makes me feel a little better, yet I'm still a little hesitant. When my hands find his arms and grip tight, he backs me up into the wall and deepens the kiss. Suddenly, my reservations go right out the window and I'm completely and utterly turned on. It's been so long since I've wanted a guy this much.

I wish I could say that it erases all the pain inside me, that the scars and memories suddenly fade away and are forgotten in an instant. But that's the thing about scars. They always stay with us, whether visible or unseen. It doesn't mean that I have to let them control me, though, so I let go and kiss him back with everything I have in me, allowing myself to momentarily forget about the terrible stuff that happened to me.

He tastes minty and I can't figure out why. All I saw him drink was Bacardi tonight, and I wonder if he popped a mint in anticipation of this moment. I find the idea cutely amusing and smile against his lips.

He pulls away slightly. "What's so funny?"

"Nothing." I chuckle again, sliding one of my hands around the back of his neck and kissing him far less timidly.

Our bodies press together and I can feel how much he wants me as he gently grinds his hips against me. God, I forgot how much I loved to kiss and touch. I get so into it I almost forget where we are. When someone drives by and honks their horn, I immediately pull away, catching my breath and trying to process what just happened.

Greyson looks like he's teetering somewhere between being high and turned on as he backs up, his mouth tugged to a lopsided grin. "So, thanks and um, yeah, I'll text you tomorrow with the details." He rakes his fingers through his hair and he kind of trips over his feet as he turns for the grass.

I smile at the sight of his awkward side coming out. "And there it is."

Seth & Greyson

He gives me a wave from over his shoulder before disappearing down the sidewalk. I turn for the door, taking a few deep breaths to calm myself down before I slip my keycard through the slot again and walk inside.

I instantly freeze when I spot Luke lounging in one of the chairs inside the entrance.

"Hey, man," he says with a chin nod.

My heart pounds in my chest and blood roars in my eardrums. Did he just see us kiss? The taste of dirt floods my mouth. *Stop thinking about it, Seth, and relax. Just breathe. Everything will be okay.* "Hey..." I glance around the empty room. "What're you doing down here?"

He shrugs, sitting up in the chair. "Well, I was going to go up to my room, but then Kayden texted me saying that Callie was spending the night and that I should crash somewhere else."

"What the fuck?" I storm for the elevator. "I told him to keep his hands off her."

Luke clumsily trips to his feet. "Would you relax?" He grabs my arm, stopping me. "He's not sleeping *with* her. He's letting her crash because of some red scarf on the doorknob or something."

"How the hell do I know that's true? I don't really know him. Or you, for that matter."

Luke pulls out his phone, taps the screen, and hands it to me. "Here, read his text. It should give you some peace of mind."

I glance down at the message.

Kayden: Hey, I'm taking Callie back to our place because there was a red scarf on her doorknob. Could you find a place to crash? She's a little nervous around people she doesn't know and I don't want her worried about anything.

"All right, that's actually kind of sweet." I hand him his phone, relaxing a little. "Where are you going to crash, though?"

Luke points at the front door. "I'm actually waiting for someone to pick me up for a party."

"Weren't you just at one?"

"Yeah, so? I want to keep the fun going. Besides, I'm not even close to being tired."

"All right, gotcha." I pull out my phone and send Callie a text to call me the moment she wakes up. "I'm actually not that tired myself."

Seth & Greyson

In fact, I'm extremely wired. My mind is racing with thoughts of Greyson's kiss and how soft his lips felt, how fucking amazing it felt to be kissed again. The idea of going to sleep seems absurdly implausible.

"You want to go out with us?" He glances at the parking lot just outside the window. "We're thinking about hitting up this place called Red Ink that's supposed to have cheap drinks and killer music."

I put my phone away. "Who are you going with?"

"A girl I met at the party," he says, looking back at me. "If you want, we can chase down Greyson and see if he wants to go, too."

I try to keep my shock under control. Luke obviously witnessed me kissing Greyson. My first kiss out in the open. My first kiss since the assault.

"You'd be okay with that?"

"Why the fuck wouldn't I be? Greyson's cool. You're cool. We're all just living one fun-filled life of coolness."

I study him closely, wondering if he's for real. He seems dead serious and kind of confused about why I'm staring at him.

I decide I'm going to do it. I've already taken a few big steps tonight, so why not just keep going? Nothing bad has happened yet. *I can do this.*

"Okay, I'm always down for clubbing." I retrieve my phone again. "I'm going to text Greyson, though, because I'm not about to run down the sidewalk after him. It goes against my lifetime vow of never exercising."

He laughs, plopping down in the chair again. "Sounds good."

I pause, thinking about what I should say in the text.

Me: Hey, so Luke Price and an unknown girl invited me to the Red Ink. He invited u, too.

I hit send and quickly type up another message.

Me: Oh yeah, I'd really like it if u went.

"How do you even know Greyson?" I ask Luke while I wait for Greyson to reply.

"We're in Bio together. He's actually my lab partner. He seems pretty cool." His attention whips to the side as headlights shine through the window. "And there's our ride." He hops to his feet and heads to the door with me following.

Seth & Greyson

By the time we reach the parking lot, Greyson hasn't text back. *Totally deserved,* I think to myself, *for blowing him off so often.*

I'm about to climb into the car when my phone vibrates. I smile as I fish it out.

Greyson: Sure. I'm down. I'm about four blocks down, but I'll turn around.

Me: No, just wait there. We'll pick u up.

I duck into the car, feeling nervous, but giddy. The giddiness remains even when I look down at my scars. Maybe, just maybe, I'll be able to conquer my fears and my past after all.

Chapter 9

Seth

"Luke, Luke, Luke," I tsk him from across the booth. "Where the hell did you find that girl? On the street corner?"

Luke glances over his shoulder at the brunette that brought us here, who grins at him and slides her hands down her body, right there for everyone at the bar to see. "She's not that bad, is she?" he asks, looking at me.

"Well, I'm not the best judge, but I'm going to go with a no." I turn my head to Greyson, who's sitting in the booth beside me. "What do you think?"

Greyson snorts a laugh as he stirs the ice in his whiskey tonic. "You think I'm a better judge than you?"

"True." I direct my attention back to Luke. "All I know is that the leopard print dress she's wearing is tacky and don't even get me started on those fishnet tights. I'd say her shoes are okay alone, but the whole outfit together," I make a gagging face. "So gross."

"So, you're basing who she is on how she looks?" Luke questions in surprise. "That's harsh."

"No, I'm basing who she is on the sole fact that she thinks the," I make air quotes, "'person' in the GPS system sounds super hot and she wonders if he's single."

"Okay, she might not be the brightest chick in the room, but she's still hot." Luke picks up his drink and swallows it in one shot.

"That's debatable," I argue, scooping up the drink in front of me.

Greyson chuckles as he slides his arm along the booth, so the crook of his elbow is resting just behind my head. Even though he's not touching, I can feel his nearness all over me. Panic flashes through me and I take a few measured breaths as I glance around the busy club. People are dry humping each other on the dance floor, flirting at the bar, and hanging out in booths. All having fun, totally relaxed, like I should be.

"She's just a hook up," Luke explains, setting down his empty glass. "It's not like I'm trying to date her or any-thing."

"Have you even dated anyone, *ever*?" I ask with doubt.

He rolls his eyes like what I said is the most absurd thing he's ever heard. "Yeah, right."

"Never once?" I question. "Not even in high school?"

With his jaw set tight, he looks out at the dance floor. "It's not my thing, okay?"

I open my mouth to press more, but Greyson brushes his finger across the back of my neck and shakes his head, signaling for me to let it go. The touch causes my mind to instantly go back to the kiss we shared earlier and I start getting wound up all over again. It makes me a bit nervous, though, being out with people.

Luke abruptly rises to his feet. "I think I'm going to go get a drink." He strides off toward the bar, pushing people out of his way.

"Are you my voice of reason now?" I ask in a low tone, leaning in toward Greyson.

Seth & Greyson

"Hey, you're the one who said you cross personal boundaries sometimes." His smile lights up his eyes. "I thought I'd help you out. He seemed a little upset."

"I wonder why."

"I'm sure he has a reason, but I don't think he wanted to talk about it."

I swish the ice around in the glass. "What about you?"

His forehead furrows. "What about me?"

I roll up my sleeves and rest my arms on the table. "How many guys did you date in high school?"

He lifts the brim of his glass to his mouth and sips a long drink before setting it back down. "You really want a number?"

I nod, even though I'm not really sure I do.

He huffs out a sigh then counts down on his fingers. "Five total."

I try to decide if that's a lot. Since he came out when he was fourteen and his parents were okay with him dating, that doesn't seem so bad. But it makes me look very pathetic and inexperienced.

117

Strands of his hair fall into his eyes as he tips his head forward and stares into his glass. "What about you?" He lifts his gaze to me and my heart slams against my chest, harder than the beat of the bass in the song playing from the sound system.

"I don't really want to tell you."

"Why not?" His lip pops out to a sexy pout. I don't think he even realizes he's doing it, which makes it even sexier.

"Because it's going to make you think I'm lame."

"I would never think you're lame."

"Yeah, we'll see." I sigh, placing a hand over my scars. "One."

His head cocks to the side. "One?"

I nod, shamefaced. "Yep, just one."

He brushes his hair out of his eyes. "I don't know why, but I thought it'd be more."

"Yeah, I grew up in a small town, so there weren't a lot of options," I explain in a tight voice. "Plus, the town I grew up in didn't make it easy. Everyone knows everyone, so I couldn't even sneak out on a date without it getting back to my mother." I sigh again. "It probably makes me sound pathetic that I just didn't say to hell with what everyone thinks."

"It's not pathetic." He covers my hand with his. "It wasn't always easy for me, either, and I had two supportive parents. I can't even imagine how hard it's been for you. Did you have any friends or anything to support you?"

My fingers flex below his and even though it's almost instinct at this point to pull away, I force myself to keep my hand where I want it to be. "I had a couple, but no one close."

"What about the guy you dated?"

I smash my lips together so forcefully I feel like they're going to bruise.

"Seth." His eyes soften and I swear he can read right through me, see the scars hidden on the inside of me, beneath my skin, along my heart, across my soul.

Tears start to burn in my eyes, but I suck them back. "Can we talk about something else? I don't think I'm ready for this conversation yet."

"Okay." He easily lets it go and I like him even more because of it.

We spend the next few hours talking and drinking. When he asks me to dance, I feel bad when I say no.

"I don't think I'm ready for that," I explain apologetically. "I'm sorry."

"That's okay." His lips tug to a small smile, covering up his disappointment. He looks at his watch and his eyes widen. "Shit, it's after three o'clock. What do you say we head back to campus?"

"I actually like that idea a lot. I'm starting to reach my sleep drunk phase." My gaze skims the dance floor, the bar, and the entrance. "But where the hell is Luke?"

"He left about an hour ago with that girl," Greyson says.

I shudder. "She was so gross. He could do way better."

Greyson smiles to himself as he gets to his feet. "I'm going to go to the bathroom and then we can go. It's a pretty nice night, anyway. Great for a walk."

By the time I guzzle down the rest of my drink, he's made it back to the booth. "You ready?"

"Yeah." I stand up and start pushing my way to the door.

Seth & Greyson

He moves up behind me, so close that his solid chest brushes my back. His body heat engulfs me and I find myself slowing down and taking my time.

The song suddenly switches to a more popular one and the crowd around us goes wild. Everyone starts jumping up and down and the floor vibrates. Greyson laughs and joins in, dancing behind me while continuing to move toward the door. Every time he moves, he grinds against me. By the time we make it to the exit doors, I'm on the verge of losing it, so riled up all I can think about is ripping his clothes off. I almost welcome the idea, too, and contemplate acting on what my body wants, even surrounded by people.

Thankfully, the cool night air acts kind of like a cold shower and helps me relax a bit. I manage to keep myself under control as we round the building and head down the sidewalk toward the campus a few miles away. It's late enough that hardly anyone's out and when Greyson reaches over and takes my hand, I don't pull away.

"You never did tell me what your major is," Greyson says as we stroll past the closed stores.

"That's because I don't have one." Between the alcohol in my system and his fingers wrapped around mine, I feel high, like I'm having a crazy out-of-body experience.

"I figure there's just too many things I'm good at to pick only one talent," I joke with a grin.

Chuckling under his breath, his gaze flicks to the stars in the sky then back at me. "If you had to pick a major right now, what would it be?"

I thrum my finger against my lip. "How about weekend partying?" I tease. "No, if I really had to pick one right now, I'd probably pick psychology."

"Really?"

"Yeah. There's something about the human mind that I find fascinating," I tell him. "But I also like English and drama and, of course, clothes, but that can't really be a major. The one subject I *hate* is math. A math major will never, *ever* happen."

"Do you play any sports?"

I choke on a laugh. "Are you kidding me?"

Greyson shrugs innocently. "I'm just trying to figure you out, and you never know."

I glance down at my stylish outfit. "Do I look like I play sports?"

"I don't know." He shrugs again. "Maybe you're hiding a rock hard body under those clothes."

I roll my eyes. "Oh, whatever. You're totally feeding me a line right now."

"I am not," he protests, biting back a grin.

I roll my eyes so hard they almost get stuck up in my head. "What about you?" I step back and scroll over his lean, toned, smoking hot body. "You could be a sports guy?"

"The only thing I do that is even remotely athletic is going to the gym."

"Aw, so you work out?" I muse over something. "I think you and I might be polar opposites."

"Is that a bad thing?"

"Nope. I don't think so, anyway. I actually told my friend Callie the day I met her that opposites attract and make the best kind of friends."

"You two seem really close," he says.

"We are… She's my best friend," I tell him. "I like helping her, too."

He momentarily studies me, his gaze making me feel restless. "Who helps you, though?"

I shrug, getting squirmy over where the conversation is headed. "I've always been good at taking care of myself. Besides, her letting me help her helps me, if that makes sense." I chuckle as I daze off at the lampposts across the street. "We have this list of things she's afraid to do. I've been helping her slowly scratch off stuff and have even done some of the stuff with her. It's fun, but I still worry about her."

"That guy she was with at the party," he says, glancing at a car as it drives by. "That's the guy she likes, right?"

I nod. "Yeah, there's a long story behind how they met, too... I think they'd be good together if they could get on the same page. But Callie's afraid and doesn't trust many people. And Kayden... Well, I don't know him very well, but from what Callie's told me, he has every right to be wary."

He grows quiet, staring at the intersection ahead of us. "I'd really like to meet her. Callie... I mean... I know she's important to you." He offers me a smile. "Maybe sometime in the future the three of us can hang out?"

"Okay." It seems like such a simple request, but it's so much more.

Seth & Greyson

He's talking about the future. Meeting my best friend. Whatever's happening between us, he sees as a long-term thing, which probably means a lot of dating, hand holding, kissing, intimacy, emotions. I won't be able to hide behind my smile anymore.

I'm not sure if I'm ready for that.

All I know is that I want it, more than I think I realized.

Chapter 10

Greyson

Friday night, I'm stupidly nervous for some reason. It's not like Seth and I haven't hung out. We've spent a lot of time together since the poker game. We hung out that night at the Red Ink, drinking well into the morning hours, and we've grabbed lunch together, been to a movie, and texted off and on each day in the week since.

Tonight's date night, and I waver between being excited and wanting to hurl as Seth and I wander past the painted canvases and photographs hanging on the walls. Maybe it's because I haven't really done much dating, and I feel a bit out of my element, my full awkwardness shining through.

Seth & Greyson

"So, this is what you do, huh?" Seth squints at a photo of a flower taken at an angle to blur the surroundings.

"In a way, kind of." I take a sip of my wine as I study him instead of the photo. "I actually prefer taking pictures of people, though."

"Oh, yes, I remember." Seth glances at me from the corner of his eye, his lips twitching upward. "When they're not watching, right?"

I shake my head, reliving the embarrassment all over again. "Actually, yes. And not just with you," I say as we move to the next exhibit, a canvas splattered with neon colors. "I think the best photos are taken when the person isn't watching. They're completely themselves and not so self-conscious."

"Yeah, I can kind of see that." He examines the painting in front of us. "No offense, but I don't really understand how splattering paint across a canvas can be art."

"No offense taken at all, since I completely agree with you." I smile at him, grab his arm, and wander toward the back corner, where a few of my photos are being displayed. "What about these? What do you think of them?"

Seth finishes the rest of his wine then angles his head to the side. "I'm not sure… they feel kind of dark and are taken at a really awkward angle."

I feel like I've been punched in the stomach. "Yeah, I guess I can see that."

Seth turns his head toward me with a sly smile on his face. "I'm fucking with you. I know they're yours."

I shake my head, but realize how much I value his opinion. "That was a dick move," I say in a light tone so he'll know I'm kidding.

"Sorry. I promise I didn't mean it, though. I just have a twisted sense of humor." He turns his concentration to the picture I took of Jenna and Ari on a bridge with the river as their background.

"They didn't know I was taking it," I explain, moving up behind him.

He tenses from my nearness, but doesn't budge. I haven't been able to stop thinking about the way he kissed me the other night. I was kind of shocked when he allowed me to kiss him, and I was completely floored when he took charge the way he did. I can't wait to kiss him again. Tonight. Tomorrow night. Kiss and kiss and kiss.

"They look so happy and in love," he remarks quietly. "And free."

"Free?"

"To be themselves." He cups his scarred arm as he stares at the picture. "I kind of envy them in a way."

"Seth." I gently place a hand on his arm. "Tell me what happened."

He shakes his head. "I can't."

"Why not? I promise, I'm a good listener. I can be there for you."

He shakes his head again. "It's too soon and honestly, I think the story's a little too dark for you. I love how you don't see all the ugly in the world... I don't want to take that away from you." Summoning a deep breath, he turns around and faces me. "So, you have to tell me what's up with that giant statue at the front door that totally looks like a penis." His subject change throws me off a bit, and it takes me a moment to get my footing again.

"Penis statue?" I scratch my head. "I'm not sure which one you're talking about?"

He aims a finger toward the front door at a tall, blue tinted sculpture.

I shake my head. "Fuck, it really does look like a penis, doesn't it?"

He laughs. "It does, but I don't think that's what it's supposed to be. The plaque on it said 'to inspire you.' It totally did, but not in the way I think it's meant to."

"Oh, yeah." I down the rest of my wine in one swallow. "How did it inspire you, then?"

"It inspired me to never, ever attempt to understand art." He peeks over his shoulder at my photos. "I like yours, though. They're the only ones I really get."

"Just wait until you see Jenna's." When intrigue crosses his face, I grab his hand and pull him toward the back of the building. On my way, I swipe two more glasses of wine from of the serving table, then duck behind a curtain that leads to the room where Jenna set up her exhibit.

Darkness surrounds us, and I smile to myself as Seth's hand tightens on mine. When Jenna told me what she was doing, I initially thought it was creepy. Now, though… Well, I think she might be fucking brilliant.

"What the hell is this?" he hisses under his breath. "I can't see a damn thing."

Seth & Greyson

"I think that might be part of the point," I whisper, sliding my hand up his arm. I feel him shiver from my touch and my cock starts to get hard. Unable to see, any reservation I felt has vanished and I feel so... alive. "Come here," I whisper, pulling him closer.

Our bodies crash together, but our lips don't quite connect, and we end up bumping foreheads. We laugh, fingers fumbling, my heart racing.

"Okay, that was *so* the worst kiss."

"No way," he says as he works to catch his breath. "I think it might quite possibly be the best kiss I've ever had."

Before I can reply, his lips find mine. Through the dark, my hands wander over his body, up his arms to his shoulders as I pull him closer. My pulse pounds as I let out a quiet moan and deepen the kiss, gripping him tightly. I've kissed plenty of guys, but this kiss is so different. I feel so comfortable, so *un*-awkward, so in my element. Right now, in this moment, is exactly where I belong. It took me a while to find it, and I'm not about to fucking let it go.

Suddenly, a bright light flashes through the room, lighting up the walls and curtains around us.

Seth jerks back, eyes wide as the lights turn on. "What the fuck was that?"

"That was perfection." Jenna jumps through the curtain with an old school Polaroid photo in her hand. "Oh, my God, that was seriously the most perfect kiss I've ever seen."

Seth's jaw is pretty much hanging to the floor. "Were you watching us?" he asks, trying to catch his breath.

"Only towards the end." She lifts the photo in front of her. "So I could take this. It's part of my exhibit. You would be amazed at how much freedom people feel when they're in a dark room and don't think anyone's watching."

"But someone *was* watching." He snatches the photo and stares at it as the white turns to color. "A creepy girl with purple hair."

"I'm sorry if I made you feel uncomfortable," Jenna says, but doesn't sound particularly apologetic. "If it makes you feel any better, I've done it to like ten other couples already. And one couple was a step away from having sex on the floor."

Seth's nose scrunches as he glances down at the carpet, but he loosens up when he looks back at the photo again. "I'll forgive you," he says. "But I'm keeping the photo."

Seth & Greyson

"You have to let me at least see it first." Jenna reaches to take the photo.

Seth tucks his arm behind his back. "No way."

Jenna pokes out her lip and clasps her hands in front of her. "*Please*."

Seth glowers at her. "You know that cutesy, innocent look isn't going to work on me, right?"

Jenna scowls at him, but then smirks. "I bet I can get you to show it to me."

"Yeah, right. You don't know who you're messing with, honey. I always get my way."

Jenna pokes my side. "Greyson, pout and tell him you want him to show me the photo."

I raise my hands in front of me. "I'm not getting into the middle of this."

She jabs me again. "You're the one who instigated the kiss, therefore this is all your fault."

"That is kind of true," he says, amused. "So, she has a valid point."

I gape at the two of them. "What kind of logic is that? And how the hell did you two go from arguing to turning on me."

"We're not turning on you." She reaches up and pinches my face between her hands. "We just want to see that cute pouty face of yours. I don't know what the big deal is. You do it all the time, anyway."

I shift my weight and move my head out of her grip. "I do not?" I glance at Seth. "Do I?"

Jenna beams brightly. "See? Now do it."

I roll my eyes, but oblige them and pout. Seth covers his mouth to hide his laughter, while Jenna claps her hands like she won a prize.

"See? Adorable," she singsongs, still clapping her hands in front of her.

I shake my head, snatch the photo from Seth, and shove it at her. "There you go." I head for the curtain. "I'm leaving before the two of you try to make me strip or something."

"I'm totally down for that," Seth calls out and Jenna busts up in a fit of giggles.

Seth & Greyson

I'm not really mad, especially since Seth seemed okay with having our picture taken. Earlier, when Jenna suggested I take Seth back there during our date, I was a little hesitant over how he'd react.

I end up waiting for Seth on the other side of the curtain. He comes out moments later, stuffing the photo into his pocket.

"Don't I at least get to see it?" I cross my arms and stick out my lip.

"In a bit," he replies in a playful tone, quickly swiping his finger across my lip. "Now, come on. Let's go get stupidly drunk on wine and make fun of that large and slightly crooked penis statue at the front."

Laughing, I follow him back over to the wine, where we both get a refill.

We spend the next couple of hours wandering around, looking at art, admiring some, but mostly just making fun of stuff. It's probably the most fun date I've ever had, and by the time we're headed back to the dorms, I don't want the night to end.

"If you want, we can go back to my place for a while," I suggest to Seth in the backseat of Ari's car.

Ari is driving and is a little grumpy about it, since he was elected DD and is now stuck chauffeuring Jenna, Seth, and I around.

Seth doesn't answer right away and I can almost feel his anxiety, even sitting a seat length away from him. I wonder exactly what he thinks I'm proposing.

"Okay... Yeah, but only on one condition." The streetlights from outside reflect in his eyes as he smiles at me.

"And what's the condition?"

"That we stop and get some ice cream. I have the drunk munchies."

"Drunk munchies? I didn't know that was a thing."

"It's kind of my thing." He scoots closer to me. "Every time I get drunk, I feel like I'm starving."

"Oh! I totally get that!" Jenna exclaims from the front seat and fist pumps the air, but ends up smacking herself in the face. "Ari, to the ice cream store!"

The three of us erupt in laughter and even Ari seems to get a kick out of it.

"I'll get you ice cream," he says, steering the car into the store parking lot. "But no more drinks for you."

Seth & Greyson

She waves him off and hops out of the car before it even comes to a full stop. The rest of us get out and chase her into the store, all the way to the frozen food section. We make our selections and I learn just how big an ice cream junkie Seth is when he chooses three flavors—mint, cookie dough, and chocolate chip.

"Please tell me you're not going to mix all three together," I say as we climb back into the car after we've paid.

"Of course I am." He smiles at me as he shuts the door. "What other way is there to eat ice cream?"

"The normal way." I buckle my seatbelt. "One flavor at a time."

"This way gives it a kick."

"Like a kick to the stomach, I bet."

Biting back a grin, he glares at me. "Because of that little remark, I'm so going to make you try it."

"No way.

"Want to bet?"

"I think the last time we bet, you lost."

"Not this time," he says. "Besides, the last time I let you win."

I choke on a laugh. "That's so not true and you know it."

"No, I *know* I know that I'm right."

"Huh?"

We exchange a confused, intoxicated look and then bust up laughing.

We continue to playfully argue during the drive home. The mood between us shifts, though, after we say goodbye to Jenna and Ari and start up the stairway toward my place.

"I bet it's nice living here," Seth remarks as he glances around the quiet apartment complex.

"It's okay." I shove the key in the lock. "I feel a little out of the loop, though." After I unlock the door, I push it open and flip on the lights. "Like all the good stuff happens at the dorms and I only hear about it while I'm in class."

"Trust me, the dorms are boring," he says, entering my place. He looks around at the sofa, the flat screen television, and the pile of photos on the coffee table. "This photography thing isn't just about the scholarship or school, is it? You like, really, *really* enjoy it." He picks up a picture I took of a garden I passed during my walk to school.

"It's kind of my version of writing tortured poetry." I shut the door and slip off my jacket. "It helps me express myself when I can't seem to verbalize how I feel."

Seth sets down the photo and reaches into his pocket, retrieving the photo Jenna took of us. He briefly assesses it before placing it down on the table.

"Can I look at it now?" I ask, coming up beside him.

He shrugs, stepping back. "Be my guest."

As I move forward to look at the picture, he walks around my small living room, checking out my collection of shot glasses, countless pictures, and DVDs. I lean down to look at the photo and smile. We look so into the kiss and all that tension Seth carries is gone. Tomorrow, I'll make sure to tell Jenna how brilliant she is.

When I stand up straight, I notice Seth is staring at a framed picture of my parents and me near the beach. It was taken on a timer, but turned out to be a pretty amazing photo.

"This is your mom and dad?" he asks quietly.

"Yeah, that was taken on the beach not too far from where I grew up."

"It's pretty... And you all look so happy." He steps back from the picture and faces me. "So, now what do we do?"

I shrug, pretending I have no idea, when really I do. I have tons and tons of fucking ideas of what the two of us could do together. "We could watch a movie or something."

Seth contemplates my offer. "I'm down for a movie just as long as it's a comedy and," a conniving grin spreads across his face, "You eat my ice cream concoction."

I make a gag face. "I seriously don't know if I can do it."

He rolls his eyes at me. "Quit being a baby." He swings around me, collects the bag of ice cream off the coffee table, then heads to the kitchen.

I follow after him and when I enter, he's opening and shutting cupboards.

"Where the hell are your bowls?" he asks through a huff.

Seth & Greyson

I open the dishwasher, grab a large red bowl and spoon, and set them down on the counter. Grinning, he opens the tubs of ice cream and scoops a spoonful of each flavor into the bowl. Once he's finished, he stirs it around, mixing it all together, and then scoots the bowl toward me.

"Dig in." He grins.

I frown at the bowl. "I find it kind of twisted that you're enjoying this so much."

"I thought we clarified at the art show that it was fun watching you pout."

I rub my hand across my face and sigh. "Fine, you win this one."

"And I thought we also clarified at the art show that I win everything," he says, fully entertained.

Shaking my head, I scoop up a spoonful of the ice cream. Then, holding my breath, I take a taste.

"So?" Seth waits eagerly for me to answer.

"It's about as disgusting as I thought." I reach for a paper towel and spit the ice cream in it.

Seth laughs in shock before turning his nose up at the contents of the bowl. "I can't believe you ate that. That looks so gross."

I lower the paper towel from my face and arch an eyebrow. "Why are you acting like you never eat this?"

"Because I don't. I mean, I'll put it all in a bowl and eat it separately, but I don't mix it together like that." He covers his mouth as he tries to silence his laughter. "I'm sorry. I honestly didn't think you would eat it."

"Now you owe me." I slide the bowl across the counter toward him. "Dig in."

His nose crinkles. "I'd rather not."

I cross my arms over my chest and lean against the counter, pretending to be more upset than I really am. "Then I'm not going to forgive you."

"Yeah, right. You're too nice not to." But he picks up the bowl, dips the spoon into the ice cream, and takes bite. He wavers as he swallows it. "It's really not that bad. Totally works for the munchies."

He eats half the bowl while I dish up my own ice cream then we wander into the living room and sit down in front of the shelf that has my DVDs on it.

Seth & Greyson

"So, a comedy, huh?" I skim the titles, searching for one I think would be good.

"I like funny movies. Life's depressing enough without spending time watching movies that suck the life from your soul."

I glance up at him and find him staring at his scars again. "Seth... I know you don't want to talk about it, but I wish you would. I can handle the ugly stuff... I know it exists."

"Knowing it exists and experiencing it are two different things... it changes you, you know?" When I don't say anything, he sets his bowl down and sighs. "I'm still not ready to tell you where the scars came from, but if you want, I can tell you a little bit about myself."

I nod, inching closer to him. "You know I want to hear it."

He blows a stressed breath as he rests back on his hands. "I used to be this really funny person."

"What do you mean *used to*? You still are."

"No, I'm different now. I mean, I'm still funny and everything, but half the time it feels like I'm running on autopilot. Jokes come naturally to me and it's easier just to laugh stuff off." He leans forward and rubs his arm. "I didn't tell my mother I was gay. She just sort of found out after… something happened. She wasn't happy at all. Told me I deserved what happened to me. She almost threw me out of the house, but after some pathetic begging on my part, she let me stay. Honestly, I wish I could've left sooner, but I didn't have anywhere to go." He shrugs. "And that's pretty much the gist of it."

My heart aches for him to the point that my chest actually hurts. "The thing that happened… does it have to do with how you got the scars on your arm?"

He nods, swallowing hard.

"Did you…" I shift my weight so that I'm facing him. "Did your mom hurt you?"

"No, it was nothing like that."

I think about asking him if it was the guy he dated. When he briefly talked about him while we were at the Red Ink, I got the sense something bad happened between the two of them.

Before I can say anything, he sits up straight and says, "Can we drop it, please? I'd rather do *anything* else than talk about my depressing life."

Seth & Greyson

I don't want to drop it at all. I want to find out who hurt him. Find out what's causing all that pain in his eyes right now. But I don't think pushing him is going to help.

"What movie do you want to watch?" I set my ice cream down. "Any one you want, I'll watch."

"I'm actually not really in the mood to watch a movie anymore," he mumbles, staring at the window just over my shoulder.

Figuring he means he wants to go back to his dorm, I start to get to my feet, even though I'm not ready for him to go. "Okay, I'll walk you."

"Greyson, that's not what I meant." Without warning, his fingers wrap around my arm and he pulls me straight down to his mouth.

I worry the kiss might be a distraction from whatever he's running from, but I get too lost in the feel of his lips to stop it. I kiss him back, our tongues tangling as he grips at my arms. My muscles flex under his hands and he constricts his grasp.

We kiss and kiss and kiss, just like I've imagined doing tons of times. Somehow, we end up lying on the floor, a mess of tangled arms and legs. I only move back to reach around and tug my shirt over my head. He follows my lead and peels his off, too.

My fingers travel over his lean muscles as he slips his hand across my abs. They tauten as his fingers start to drift downward to the button of my jeans. I realize where this is heading, but I'm not sure I want to go there yet. In the past, I rushed into the physical aspects of a relationship without really taking the time to get to know someone. I probably know Seth better than I know anyone else, but it still feels like there's so much more to discover.

"I think..." I'm so wound up that I can barely get the words out. "I think maybe we should..."

"Yeah, we should..." Seth breathes between the kisses, grasping onto me tighter.

At first, I think he's misunderstanding me, but then he pushes away. He rolls onto his back and stares up at the ceiling, gasping for air. His eyes are huge and flooded with panic as he places a hand on his forehead.

I rotate on my side and prop up on my elbow. "Are you okay?"

His gaze glides to me. "I'm fine, I just... I need to take things a little slower." He sits up, grabs his shirt, and pulls it on. "Can we watch that movie now... or I can go home if you want. I don't want to be sitting here, bugging you with my awkwardness."

I reach for my shirt. "Seth, I think we already established that I'm the awkward one." When he meets my gaze, I wink at him, trying to alleviate the tension in the air.

His shoulders relax as a laugh slips from his lips. "Oh yeah, I completely forgot about that. Guess I'll have to settle for second best, then."

"Guess so." I slip my shirt over my head, grab a movie from the shelf, and pull him up. "I know you said you weren't in the mood, but I promise this is a good one."

When he gets to his feet, he plops down on the sofa. "I'll stay for one, but then I should probably head back."

"Sounds good." I pop the DVD in and settle on the sofa beside him as the movie clicks on.

Halfway through the movie, Seth dozes off on my shoulder. Instead of waking him up, I grab a blanket from the floor, lie down with him, and wrap my arms around him, simply holding him. I've never been in love before, but as the most calming feeling settles over me as I start to fall asleep, I have to wonder if maybe this is it.

Jessica Sorensen

Chapter 11

Seth

The next few weeks drift by in a daze of autumn colors
and new fall wardrobes. Greyson and I spend a lot of time
together, studying and hanging out at his place, but I still
haven't introduced him to Callie, nor have we done anything more than kiss. Crossing that bridge means making a
commitment to Greyson, which goes hand-in-hand with
opening my heart up to him. I don't think I'm ready for
that, especially when I can't even hold his hand in public
without going into a full-blown anxiety attack.

Even though Greyson insists he's okay with how
things are proceeding, I can tell it bothers him every time I
let go of his hand, move back from a kiss, or slide away
from him in the seat.

Seth & Greyson

"You look sad... What's wrong? Is it because you have to go home tomorrow?" Callie asks one day while we're studying in the library.

Thanksgiving is this week, so most of the campus has cleared out. Everyone is excited to be going home for the holidays. Me, not so much. In fact, I'd stay here, but my mother's forcing me to go back and suffer through a mind-numbing week of Mapleville gossip and family drama.

I force a cheery smile. "I'm fine. I was just spacing out."

She chews on the end of her pen while eyeing me perceptively. "Seth, I know you love helping me, but I want to be there for you sometimes, too. It feels good when I'm able to help you and makes me feel like less of a taker."

"Taker?"

"Yeah, the kind of person that's always taking and never gives anything in return. You're always giving, giving, giving, and I'm taking, taking, taking."

"I like giving stuff to you." My eyes trail over the shelves and front desk of the quiet library before I shut my textbook and fold my arms on top of it. "But if you really want to know what's bothering me... It's Greyson."

She drops her pen on the table and tucks a strand of her shoulder-length brown hair behind her ear. "Are you mad at him or something?"

"No, it's nothing like that." I fiddle with the thin leather bracelet around my wrist. "It's… what happened with Braiden. It's affecting how I react to Greyson. I know I can trust him, but I can't seem to let go and be comfortable with who I am when we're around people."

She shoves her books aside and rests her elbows on the table. "Have you talked to him about this?"

I trace the thin scars crisscrossing my arm and hand. "No… I haven't even told him about Braiden."

"Seth, I know it's hard to really open up to someone, but," she slides her arm across the table, grabs my hand, and gives it a squeeze, "It's like you're always telling me. You can't let the past own you. If you want to move forward, especially with Greyson, you're going to have to start by telling him what happened to you."

"I know I do." I free a trapped breath. "But I'm afraid."

"Of what?"

"Of… opening myself up like that again and getting broken. Besides, Greyson's so good, you know. He has these really amazing parents who have always been there for him and he's had a pretty good life. I don't want to taint that for him by bringing my shitty life into the mix."

"Seth, look at me." She tugs on my arm until I finally meet her gaze. What I see startles me. My tiny, shy Callie has turned into an intense firecracker. "You don't have a shitty life anymore. Yes, shitty stuff happened to you and yes, your mother is a… bitch." She looks guilty for saying the curse word, which makes me smile. "But you have me, Greyson, Luke, and even Kayden, and we all care about you because you're a good person worth caring for." By the time she's finished, she's so worked up she's gasping for air.

I raise my free hand in front of me. "Easy there, my little sparkler, before you explode."

"I just want you to be happy," she says, gripping onto my hand. "And I hate Braiden and all those stupid guys that did this to you. You don't deserve to be afraid all the time. You deserve to be the Seth I get to see and love."

"I love you too, baby girl." I smile at her and she returns my smile wholly. "How did you get to be so wise?"

"Hmmm…" She taps her finger against her lips. "I must have had a really great teacher, I guess."

"Must have."

"He's actually the best there is."

"Sounds like a great guy," I reply with a hint of amusement. "What's his number? Maybe I'll give him a call."

We giggle then sit back in our chairs. Outside the window, the setting sun paints the sky with pinks and golds.

"What time is it?" I check the clock on my phone then scoot back from the table. "Shit, I was supposed to meet Greyson like fifteen minutes ago."

Callie stands up and gathers her books in her arms. "You better talk to him tonight; otherwise, I'm going to add it to the list and make you."

"I'll see what I can do." But just thinking about it sends my stomach dancing, and not the good kind of dancing, either. The flailing arms, bobbing head, offbeat kind of dancing. "What about you? Have any plans for tonight?" I waggle my eyebrows suggestively as we exit the library and step outside into the cool fall air.

Seth & Greyson

She casually shrugs, tucking her books under her arm. "I might meet up with Kayden later."

I playfully bump my shoulder into hers. "You two have been spending a lot of time together."

She fights back a silly grin. "We're just friends."

"Friends with benefits."

Her cheeks flush as she avoids my gaze. "We haven't had... sex yet."

I slam to a halt in the middle of the grass. "*Yet*? That means you've been thinking about it."

Her blush spreads across her face as she stops in front of me and stares out at the street. "I didn't mean it like that."

"But you've thought about it?" I try to hide my excitement, but the fact that she's thought about it means she's making progress.

"Sometimes... but it seems so... I don't know. I just never planned on ever feeling this way about a guy."

"Kayden's a good guy." And I mean it.

Not too long ago, Callie told Kayden about how she was raped, and he's been nothing but kind, considerate and understanding with her. That makes the guy cool in my book, which is a pretty damn fabulous book and kind of hard to earn a place in.

She plucks strands of her hair out of her mouth before looking at me again. "I don't even know what I'm doing... I mean, he's so experienced and I'm..." She gestures at herself and shrugs.

"What? Gorgeous? Kind? Smart? Funny?" I slip my arm around her and start toward the parking lot. "Any guy would be lucky to have you."

She slides her arm around my back and gives me a hug. "You, too." We break apart at the front of my car and she backs up toward the dorms, pointing her finger sternly at me. "Now tell Greyson. I know it'll make you feel better."

I wave at her and climb into the car, crossing my fingers that she's right.

***

"I can't believe we're not going to see each other for an entire week," I sulk as I rummage through Greyson's fridge. We're spending our last night together before we head back to our homes. I grab a beer, bump the fridge door shut with my hip, and pop the top of the bottle. Taking a swig, I shiver from the bitter taste. "You really need to get something besides beer."

"What? Like those disgusting fruity drinks you were drinking the other day?" he teases from the sofa. He's got his arms folded and the short-sleeved shirt he's wearing makes his biceps looking amazing.
"Hey, those aren't half bad." I drop down on the sofa beside him and lean forward to glance over the stack of DVDs on the coffee table. "Which one are we watching tonight?"

His eyes are fixed on me, watching my every move so intently that I'm almost afraid to look up at him. "Your pick."

"Hmmm…" I skim my finger over the titles. "I'm not really sure what I'm in the mood for. Definitely not an action, but that's a given. Not a romance… not a comedy."

Greyson lets out a low chuckle. "It sounds like you're not in the mood for a movie."

I think about what Callie urged me to do and her promise to put it on the list if I didn't tell Greyson tonight. I know once the task makes it on the list, she's going to bug me until I complete it because that's what I do with her.

Taking a deep, shaky breath, I shift my weight and turn in the seat, bringing my leg onto the cushion. "I actually thought we could talk for a bit?"

"Talk about something specific?" he questions. "Or just talk, *talk*."

I recline against the armrest, trying to get comfortable. "Talk about something specific."

Something in my tone must warn him that we're about to have a serious talk because he rotates toward me and gives me his undivided attention. "All right, I'm all yours for the night. Talk away."

My stomach does the bad dance moves again, and I seriously wish I had an antacid or something, because I feel like I'm one foul taste away from barfing up beer. My gaze falls to the scars on my arm. The tiny white marks seem so insignificant, but I feel like they're a brand, blazing for the entire world to see.

"It's about my scars…" I trace my fingertip along the longest one, the one Braiden left when he stomped on my arm, crushing it into the dirt alongside my heart. "And about Braiden."

"Can I ask… Who's Braiden?" Greyson questions cautiously.

Seth & Greyson

I summon another breath, and then force myself to look at him. "He's the guy I used to date."

He swallows hard, his gaze trailing over my arm before returning to mine, his eyes full of sympathy. A beat of silence goes by, and my heart dances like a lunatic inside my chest.

"I'm not sure how much of the story you want to hear," I mutter. "I can give you the short version, if you want. It might be easier to take."

"Easier to take?" He scoots across the sofa until our knees touch. "Seth, I'm not afraid of your past... It just hurts to imagine you being in that kind of pain, that a guy you cared about caused those scars."

"Braiden didn't act alone," I explain. "His friends were there, too. They never really liked me, anyway."

"That doesn't make it any better."

"I'm not saying it is... I'm just saying there were other people there and I didn't care about any of them except..." I force down the lump welling in my throat and lower my head, staring at my hands. "Except Braiden."

Greyson cups my face between his hands and forces me to look at him. "What did he do to you?"

The compassion in his eyes makes it easier to open my mouth and spill my soul. If I look too deeply, though, I see something else. Love, maybe. And that… Well, that makes me afraid. Blindly, breathlessly afraid, yet at the same time, I feel completely safe.

"We'd been seeing each other for a few months, using the excuse that I was his tutor to hook up while we were supposed to be studying. Braiden was… Well, he was the popular jock loved by all and completely heterosexual to everyone but me. Even though I hadn't came out to my mother yet, there were kids at school who realized I'm gay. Word got around that Braiden and I were seeing each other." I roll my eyes. "Because that's what happens in Mapleville. When Braiden's friends found out, they confronted him and he, of course, denied it. They told him to prove it and the proof they wanted was my blood on all their hands." I shrug because I can't think of anything else to say. "And there you go."

"Seth." His voice carries a gentleness to it, as if he's afraid I'm about to break.

I realize I'm crying. "Oh, my God, this is so embarrassing." I reach up to wipe the tears away, but he holds my face firmly in his hands.

Seth & Greyson

"You should never be embarrassed for being who you are." His words strike my heart, but I nearly fall apart when he wipes my tears away with his fingertips.

"I just want to forget it ever happened... But I have all these scars on my arm that won't allow it... It's why I'm so afraid to be with you. Like *be* with you, be with you."

"God, I hate that they did this to you," he says as he finishes drying my tears. "I wish I could make it go away somehow. Tell me what to do. *Please.*"

"I wish you could make it go away, too, but unfortunately you can't... You can make it better for a little while, though."

"How?"

Without giving a verbal answer, I lean forward and smash my lips to his. With a gasp, he splays his fingers across my cheeks and opens his mouth, deepening the kiss. At first I take my time, kissing him slowly, savoring each movement of his tongue, the warmth of his skin when I run my hands up his arms. The best part about it all is the sense of security I feel. I never felt this safe with Braiden. It was always, "Shut and lock the door. I don't want anyone finding out about us."

As I lie down on the sofa, Greyson moves over me, covering my body with his. I run my fingers through his hair, tugging hard, and bite at his lip. He groans, grinding against me, and my pulse quickens in both fear and excitement at the feel of him. The slow, teasing burn suddenly shifts to uncontrollable want and I get rock hard inside my jeans. I tug off his shirt and pull him closer, never wanting to let him go.

"Seth," he whispers through ragged breaths when I trail my hand down his sexy-as-hell stomach.

"You know, you made it sound like you went to the gym every so often." I trace his muscles with my fingers. "But I'm thinking you must be one of those people who are workout psychotic."

"Maybe… just… a… little…" He seems severely distracted as I fiddle with the button of his jeans.

I mess around with the button just a bit longer before I undo it, drag down his zipper, and slip my hand down his boxers. He groans when I grasp him, rocking into me. I get lost in the feel of him as I move my hand up and down, getting more turned on by the second.

I raise my head to kiss him, but he pushes back, grabbing the bottom of my shirt and jerking it over my head. He rolls over beside me and I move with him, confused about his intent until he undoes the button of my jeans and gives me exactly what I'm giving him.

I don't know how to react. Braiden was never like this with me. He was always a taker and I the giver. I think about telling Greyson that, that he's the only guy that's ever touched me like this, but my lips can't seem to function.

I'm not sure how I went from being afraid to kiss and tell my secrets to pouring my heart out and being with him like this. My mind is racing so quickly I can't keep up, and rather than getting lost in my own head, I cling to Greyson, holding tight all the way to the end.

After things settle down, we lie on the sofa with our foreheads pressed together.

"You okay?" he asks as he struggles to catch his breath.

My heart is trying to beat its way out of my chest as I nod. "I'm more than okay... I'm perfect."

When I say it, I realize how much truth those words carry and how long it's been since I felt this way about someone. In fact, I don't think I ever have. Whatever I'm feeling is completely new and raw and terrifying, but in the best way possible.

I just hope that I can hold onto it.

Chapter 12

Seth

Going home. Le sigh. What can I say about that other than it's absolute, one hundred percent suckage? My mother is pretending I'm the son she wishes she had, telling every relative that came over for dinner that I fell in love with a girl at college and that I'm majoring in math, of all things. It's annoying and degrading and I'm one step away from screaming at the top of my lungs who I'm really seeing. I swear to God, I'm going to do it right here in the middle of Thanksgiving dinner.

"Seth, did you hear what your grandmother said?" my mom asks from across the table covered with pies, side dishes, and a turkey.

I look up from my plate and shake my head. "But it doesn't matter since she can't even hear *with* her hearing aide."

My grandmother smiles at me, confusion swirling in her eyes, while my mother looks she's contemplating stabbing me with her fork.

"Watch it, young man," she warns, cutting a piece of turkey. "I'm not going to tolerate your attitude."

"Then I guess I better not talk." I stab my fork into my salad, stuff my mouth full, and sarcastically grin at her.

She glares at me, but not wanting to cause a scene, drops the conversation and focuses on my aunt, who's getting ready to marry husband number five.

After dinner, the family gathers into the living room to reminisce. Half the stories are either embellished, complete bullshit, or just plain dull. Bored out of my mind, I decide to text Callie and see if her trip home is going any better.

Me: Hey, darling. How's it going? Good, I hope. Did you eat some delicious treats?

Callie: Maybe… But what kind of treats r u talking about?

Me: OMFG!!! Did u? Because I had this really weird feeling that you did.

Callie: Did what?

Me: U know what.

When she doesn't answer me back, I can't help but smile. She's come so far from the girl I met back in the summer and I wish I could be there to hug her or something. Honestly, what I wish is that I could be as brave as she is, say to hell with fear, flip it the bird, and put myself out there for the world to see. Whatever happens, happens and I'd be able to handle it. Instead, I'm sitting in a living room filled with people who believe I'm a math major dating a girl named Sally.

Swiping my finger over the screen, I start a new message.

Me: Hey! How's the vacation going?

Greyson: Mine's going good. I'm actually sitting on the beach right now.

Me: That's so not fair. I'm jealous :(

Greyson: If it makes you feel better, I'm thinking about u. Have been ever since I got here.

Me. Ha, ha, you're such a sap. JK, I've been thinking about u, too.

Greyson: What are u doing right now?

Me: Sitting in the living room, listening to my mother tell fake stories about my college life.

Greyson. Seth... I'm so sorry.

Me: It's not your fault. It's my own damn fault for letting her. I just want to stand up and scream the truth.

Greyson: It has to be hard when it's your own mother. I can't even imagine. I can't imagine a lot of stuff that you've gone through. You're so strong.

Me: Yeah, right. If I was strong then I'd tell everyone the truth.

Greyson: It's okay to be scared, Seth... I still am sometimes.

Me: Really??? U don't seem like it.

Greyson: It's not often, but sometimes when I hear someone say something stupid, I get a little uneasy.

Me: How do u deal with it so well? Because I'm dying to know.

Seth & Greyson

Greyson: Honestly, I just shrug it off. Even though it's hard, in the end it doesn't really matter what other people think of you, as long as you're happy. Life's too short, you know, to let other people drag you down.

Me: Wow, you're like super wise. Seriously. Maybe u should be the psych major.

Greyson. Yeah, that'd go well. I may be able to talk to you, but when it comes to complete strangers, I'm not as smooth.

Me: So u used all your smoothness on me, huh?

Greyson: Obviously. I just can't help it. You're too adorable.

A ridiculously goofy smile takes over my face as I move my fingers to type back.

"Seth, who are you texting?" my mother asks, interrupting me. "Oh. Is that Sally?"

I bite down on my lip and clench my phone in my hand as something snaps inside me. I think about what Greyson said. He's so right. Life's way too short to keep living like this.

I glance at the faint scars on my hand, the ones my mother made me cover up, and it fuels me with enough rage to stand up and confront her in a room full of people.

"Actually, that was Greyson," I tell her. "You know, my boyfriend I met at college."

Her face drains of color as her fingers strangle the cup she's holding. "He's kidding," she says to everyone with an off-pitch laugh.

"No, I'm not." My voice shakes, but I manage to stand firm. "And you know it. You've known it for a while now."

"Shut your mouth," she snaps, slamming the glass down on the table in front of her.

""No, I'm not going to stay silent anymore," I reply, my voice growing firmer. "This is who I am and you're going to either have to accept it or stop forcing me to come home."

It grows so quiet you could hear a pin drop. One of my uncles chokes on a cough and my aunt starts crying.

My mother trembles with rage as she rises from her chair and points to the door. "Get out of my house."

"Gladly." My legs shake as I pick up my coat and storm out the door. "Fuck," I curse when I realize my car's blocked in.

Having nowhere else to go, I slip on my coat and start walking down the icy sidewalk. The air has a nip to it and a layer of snow covers the grass. Goosebumps dot my arms and my teeth chatter, but I continue moving until finally I reach the gas station about a mile away. Inside, the place is practically empty. Even the tiny diner at the back has a total of zero customers. Taking a seat at one of the tables, I pull out my phone to text Greyson, but realizing how much I need to hear his voice, I end up dialing his number instead.

"Hey," he says as he picks up. "I was just thinking about you."

I slump back in the seat. "That's because I'm hard to forget."

"What's wrong?" he asks immediately. "And don't say nothing. I can tell by your voice there's something wrong."

I blow out a breath. "So, remember how when we were texting, I said I wanted to scream the truth to everyone?"

"Oh, my God, you did?" He sounds worried.

"Well, not so dramatically, but yeah, I kind of declared to everyone that I was dating you."

He hesitates before he asks, "And what happened?"

"Pretty much what I thought would happen." I trace the cracks in the table. "My mother threw me out."

"Seth, I'm so sorry. I wish I was there with you... But I'm really proud of you."

"Thanks." I glance out the window as snow begins to fall. "I think I'm going to drive back to school tonight."

"I don't like the idea of you on the road that late. Or spending the weekend by yourself," he says. "Isn't there somewhere you can crash until Sunday?"

"My car." I sigh tiredly. "It's better if I go back. Being here... It brings up too much painful shit."

"Well, if you do, call me while you're on the road and I'll talk to you during the drive."

"You know it's like a three-hour drive, right?"

"What? I can talk for three hours straight," he says and I snort skeptically. "Okay, well, you can, then."

"Sounds good... God, I can't wait until Monday when everything goes back to normal." I peer over my shoulder as the door dings and someone walks in. When I see who it is, my sullen mood sinks further. "And the day just keeps on getting shittier."

"What do you mean?"

"I mean, Braiden just walked in." I don't know why I'm so surprised. Mapleville is a small town. I should have known there was a chance I'd cross paths with him.

"Huh? Where the hell are you?"

"At a gas station." I rise from the chair as Braiden spots me.

He freezes in front of the cash register with a deer in the headlights look on his face.

"Don't hang up on me," Greyson begs anxiously. "Just walk out of there, okay? Seth, are you listening to me?"

"Yeah, I'm listening." I keep my eyes on Braiden.

He looks the same; tall, muscular, with brown hair that matches his eyes. I'm sure he's still fucking hot, but right now all I can see is the anger he had in his eyes when he tried to break me.

My pulse is racing so quickly I feel like I'm one step away from dropping dead. Somehow I manage to put one foot in front of the other and move toward the door.

Braiden glances over his shoulder at the cashier, who's reading a magazine and chomping on her gum. He relaxes a bit as he turns around and gives me a tense smile. "Hey."

My scars pulsate as I force words out of my mouth. "Are you *serious*?"

His expression drops. "Huh?"

"You seriously think you can speak to me?" I wrap my fingers around the door handle. "You have no right to talk to me anymore. You made that decision six months ago."

"Seth, if you'd just talk to me, I could explain myself. What happened… I didn't have a choice."

"Everyone has a *choice*," I snap. "You made yours the moment you showed up in that truck with your so-called friends. And trust me, I regret my *choice* of not reporting what you guys did to me to the police. "

"What the hell did you expect me to do? Tell them the truth?" he hisses, stepping toward me.

Seth & Greyson

I raise my hand in front of me. "I'm not going to get into this with you. I don't want to talk to you, see you, or have anything to do with you ever again. I'm so over it."

"Seth," he starts, but I don't want to hear it.

Turning my back on him, I push open the door and step into the flurry of snow drifting from the sky.

"Are you still there?" Greyson asks as I hike across the parking lot.

"Yeah, I'm still here." My breath puffs out in front of my face. "I'm headed back home to get my stuff and hit the road. Stay on the phone with me for a little while, though, okay?"

"Of course," he says like it's the easiest thing to do. "You know I'm always here for you."

I shuffle through the snow toward the neighborhood where I grew up. "I know you are."

Even after all the drama of the day, I manage to smile as the truth warms all the cold around me. It may feel like I'm completely alone right now, but I'm not. Callie was right. I do have people in my life that love me for who I am.

Chapter 13

Greyson

"What's with the frown, my beautiful little boy?" My mother is melting butter in a pan on the stove as I enter the kitchen, preparing to cook her favorite brownies.

Every room in the house has its own unique style, and the kitchen is no exception. Painted on the far wall is a mural of the beach. The rest of the walls are blue to match and the cupboards are yellow like the sun. It's a little strange, but somehow it works.

"Nothing." I move beside her and stare at the sizzling butter. "Need any help?"

She glances up from the pan with worry on her face. "Greyson, don't lie to me. I can tell when there's something bothering my little boy."

Seth & Greyson

"I wish you'd stop calling me that." I lean against the counter. "I'm almost nineteen."

"Oh, the big nineteen." She holds up her hands in front of her, mocking me. When a laugh escapes me, she lowers her hands, satisfied. "Just so you know, you'll always be my little boy, even when you're ninety."

I don't point out that she more than likely won't be around when I'm ninety, since it would lead to a very long story about how she'll find me in her next life.

She picks up a spoon and stirs the bubbling butter. "Tell me what's wrong."

I open the cupboard, grab a glass, and fill it with water. "It's Seth. That guy I told you about? Some stuff happened while he was at home and he left to go back to school early."

I take a sip of water, trying not to think about Seth enduring the rest of the holiday alone on campus, trying to work through what happened by himself. It hurts thinking about him being alone after all that horrible shit happened while he was at home.

"I hope everything's okay." She reaches to turn down the temperature of the burner.

"I'm not so sure that he is, even though he says he's fine."

"Can I ask what happened?" she asks, wiping her hands on a towel.

I blow out my breath and recap all the details that I know. By the time I'm finished, I feel sick to my stomach, thinking about what he must be going through right now and how badly I wish I was by his side.

"That poor boy. To go through all that… And shame on his mother. Mothers are supposed to love their children unconditionally and always be there for them." My mom moves the pan off the stove and takes my hands in hers. "If you're really serious about this boy, you should bring him home with you during your next holiday. I don't want him spending Christmas alone or, worse, at his house where he can't possibly feel safe." She reacts exactly the way I knew she would.

Although she might be a little on the crazy side, I'm lucky to have her as a parent.

"I think… Or I've been thinking that maybe I could fly back early."

She doesn't say anything. Instead, she opens my hand and studies the lines of my palm. "As much as I hate the thought of us cutting down our time together, I think you should go back early, too, and be there for Seth."

"Is that what the lines say?" I joke.

"They do," she replies, deadly serious. "Just like my dream told me you were going to meet someone new when you went off to school. You should know by now that my predictions are always right." She closes my hand. "Go pack your stuff and I'll see if I can get you on a flight."

"Thanks, Mom." I wrap my arms around her. "And I mean for everything. For not kicking me out of the house. For supporting me through everything. For making me feel okay about being who I am."

"You're welcome, honey." She kisses me on the cheek. "I love you."

"I love you, too." I pull back and head to my room, eager to pack my stuff—eager to get to Seth.

***

Ten hours later, I'm walking up to Seth's dorm building. I haven't been able to get ahold of him, so as soon as I dropped off my bags at my apartment, I headed straight to the dorms. I try his number again, but it goes straight to voicemail.

I rush across the frosted grass. Snowflakes are lightly falling from the grey sky and sprinkle the tree branches. The scene would make a great picture, but I don't have my camera with me. Plus, I have this dire urge to get to Seth's room and make sure he's okay.

When I get to the locked entrance door, I cup my hands around my eyes and peer through the glass. I spot a few people hanging out in the lounge area and knock on the door. A girl glances in my direction, gets up, and lets me in.

I brush the snow out of my hair as I step inside and head toward his room at the end of the hallway. Stopping at his door, I knock loudly since someone has the music cranked up.

Moments later, the music stops and Seth opens the door.

He takes one look at me and his jaw drops. "What are you doing here? I thought you weren't flying home until Sunday."

"Yeah, I left early." I run my fingers through my damp hair. "I thought you might need some company after what happened."

Seth & Greyson

He rubs his lips together as his gaze scrolls up and down my body. "You didn't have to do that? I know how excited your mom was to see you."

"She was fine with me coming back," I reassure him. "In fact, it was her idea."

He stares at me for a second or two, then reaches for my hand and yanks me into his cluttered room. Energy drink cans litter the floor and candy wrappers cover his bed.

"Did you go on a sugar binge or something?" I turn in a circle in the small space between the two twin beds, examining his messy room.

"I didn't feel like going out and eating alone," he says, closing the door. "I honestly planned on locking myself in here the whole weekend and binging on sugar and vodka, but then I didn't have any vodka, so," he shrugs, "I took to the energy drinks."

I notice how beaten down he's acting and how his eyes are rimmed with red. I think he's been crying and it rips open my heart. Before I even realize what I'm doing, I wrap him in my arms and pull him against me.

Jessica Sorensen

"I'm so sorry I wasn't there for you," I say as I hug him tightly. "I'm here now, though."

He rests his face in the crook of my neck as he grips the bottom of my shirt. "It's not your fault you weren't there. And it's not like I knew the shit was going to hit the fan. Besides, I made the choice to open my mouth and say what I did."

"Don't ever regret that."

"I don't."

We hug for a little longer before stepping back. He wipes his eyes with the sleeve of his shirt then blows out a breath. "So, now that you're here, do you want to go get something to eat?" He makes a face at all the candy wrappers around the room. "I've eaten so much junk food, I swear to God I can literally feel my teeth rotting out of my head."

"Whatever you want to do, the day is yours," I tell him, zipping up my jacket.

He retrieves his coat from his unmade bed. "You might want to be careful giving me that kind of freedom. God knows where the hell we'll end up." He slips his arms through the sleeves, collects his wallet and keys from the

180

Seth & Greyson

dresser, and then pulls open the door. "Wait, how did you even get in here without a keycard?"

"A couple of people were downstairs and they let me in," I explain as he locks up his room before we head down the hallway. "I tried to call you like a thousand times, but you didn't answer."

"Oh, yeah. I forgot I turned it off." He waves at one of the girls in the lounge before shoving open the outside door.

The snow has picked up and thick snowflakes fall from the sky, making it hard to see anything.

"Why'd you turn it off?" I ask, tucking my hands into my jacket pockets.

"Because my mother kept sending me texts."

"Apologies, I hope."

He lets out a hollow laugh as he kicks the tip of his boot at the snow on the ground. "Yeah, right. More like threats."

I stop under the shelter of a tree and grab his arm, forcing him to look at me. "She's threatening you?"

He shrugs it off. "It's nothing I haven't heard. I can't ever come home again. Blah, blah, blah." He rolls his eyes, pretending to be unaffected.

"I'm sorry, but your mother's a bitch."

"Oh, that she is." He pulls the hood of his jacket over his head. "Can we talk about something else, though? I promise I'm not running away from the problem. I just need a break from it."

"You're okay, though, right?" I question, knowing I'd be anything but *okay* had I suffered everything he's been through.

"Oddly enough, I kind of am. Between telling my mother off and confronting Braiden, I have this strange sense of closure. Like I've made peace with what I can't change and I feel like I'm ready to move on."

I give his hand a squeeze. "You know I'm here if you ever need to talk, vent, punch something, whatever."

He chuckles, his eyes lighting up for the first time since I walked into his room. "Punch something?"

"Yeah, as a way to get it out. You'd be surprised how therapeutic it can be."

Seth & Greyson

"Thanks for the offer, but physically exerting myself doesn't sound like much fun. I would, however, love to go dancing. I haven't done that in a while."

"Okay," I respond, unsure as to whether he wants me to accompany him since he's been so hesitant about it in the past.

"I definitely need to get something to eat first." He pats his stomach. "I'm starving."

I nod my head toward the parking lot. "Let's go, then. Like I said, the day is yours."

We hike across the snow for the car, our shoes crunching against the frostbitten grass. The snowfall is thinning, making it easier to see. When I notice a couple of guys heading up the sidewalk, I'm prepared for Seth to pull his hand out of mine, like he always does when we're around other people, but as the guys get closer, he only grips tighter. I can feel his anxiety when his palm starts to sweat and his pulse begins hammering against my fingertips, and though his gaze remains locked on his snow-covered car, he keeps glancing at the guys out the corner of his eye.

A few of them look in our direction and openly stare, but, thankfully, no one opens their mouth and we make it to the car without any problems. The last thing Seth needs is for drama to unfold during his first attempt at putting himself out there.

"Where should we eat?" Seth's fingers tremble as he fumbles to get the keys in the ignition.

"Hey, just breathe." I settle my hand on his arm to steady him. "You did good."

When his gaze meets mine, he nods unsteadily, and I can't help myself. I lean over and kiss him and he kisses me back, almost in desperation, sliding his tongue into my mouth. He hasn't shaved in a few days and I can feel his stubble under my hand as I rub his cheek and press him closer.

"I missed you," I say when I pull back, a little breathless.

"I missed you, too," he admits, backing out of the parking space.

"My mom said you should come to Florida with me for Christmas," I tell him. "But I have to warn you, you'll likely spend most of the visit getting your palm read, your cards read, and your dreams interpreted."

"That sounds fun."

"So, you'll come?"

Seth & Greyson

He scratches his forehead then flips the wipers on high speed. "Yeah, that actually sounds nice." His voice shakes nervously. "I hope they like me, though."

"Of course they will." I buckle my seatbelt and relax back in the seat. "In fact, I'm pretty sure my mom already does."

"How? She's never even met me."

"She says I seem happy and gave you the credit for that."

He smiles at this, looking a little baffled.

We spend the next couple hours eating dinner and searching for a club that's open on a holiday weekend, which turns out to be an unsuccessful endeavor. Every club worth going to is closed, so we end up heading to my apartment and playing a drinking game. Five or six shots in, my veins are buzzing with just enough alcohol that I decide it's a good idea to crank up some music and turn my living room into a club.

We start dancing, laughing and grinding our hips, feeling each other's bodies, and the laughter quickly turns to a heavy make out session. Shirts and jeans get stripped off and somehow we make it into the bedroom. Things start to get extremely hot, and I have no intention of stopping until I spot the fear on Seth's face.

"Should I stop?" I ask through ragged breaths.

His chest crashes into mine as he fights to breathe. "I just need a moment."

Nodding, I push back and sit down on the edge of the bed. Gripping onto the mattress, I struggle to get air into my lungs, trying to calm myself the fuck down.

"I'm sorry," Seth mutters from behind me.

"No, you're fine." I suck in another breath before rotating around, and I instantly regret facing him. He's still wearing only his boxers, his blonde hair is sticking up all over the place, and I instantly get hard.

"I just needed to calm down," I say in a strained voice. "You have me all riled up."

A trace of amusement turns up the corners of his lips, but the smile promptly falters. "I haven't been completely honest with you about certain stuff. I wasn't really planning on telling you and I'm not even sure I need to… But since this week has been all about the truth, I think I'm just going to be up front about my past." He crosses his legs and gets situated on the bed, growing quiet as I wait for him to proceed.

The longer he sits there silently, the more restless I feel about what the hell he's going to say.

"Last week, when we were messing around on your couch… That's the farthest I've ever been," he stares down at his hands in his lap. "I mean, I did stuff to Braiden, but he refused to do anything to *me*. He said it was because he wasn't into it, but I could tell that sometimes he wanted to. Looking back, I'm guessing it was because he was scared to go all the way… I wish I'd said something, but I was stupid back then."

"You weren't stupid. You just weren't given a real chance to see that there was an option other than hiding behind closed doors."

He dazes off over my shoulder. "I thought I was in love with him." When his eyes land on me, he shakes his head. "Clearly, I understand now that I wasn't, but back then… I don't know… This is going to sound so cliché, but I think I was looking for love in all the wrong places." His brows knit. "What about you? I know you've dated way more than I have, but have you ever been in love?"

I shake my head. "No, I never got close enough to anyone to feel that much for them." Until now.

I realize right then and there that I'm pretty sure I'm in love with Seth. I should have known the moment I dropped everything and flew back early just to make sure he was okay. It terrifies me, but in a really good way. I open my mouth to tell him so, but my phone rings from inside the apartment somewhere.

"Where the hell did I leave it?" I mutter to myself as I climb off the bed.

I stumble through the room and track the ringing to the hallway, where my phone is lying on the floor. I pick it up and see an unknown number on the screen.

"Hello?" I answer, putting the phone up to my ear as I make my way back into the bedroom.

Seth is lounging on my bed with his arms tucked behind his head, smiling at me contently. I have this overwhelming urge to throw the phone down and scream that I love him.

"Hey, Greyson... It's Callie. Sorry to bug you... Seth used my phone once to call you and I found the number in my log." She sounds choked, as if she's been crying. "I don't mean to bother you, but Seth won't answer his phone and I really need to talk to him." A heart-wrenching sob fills the line.

"Yeah, he's right here. Hold on." I quickly hand him the phone and mouth, *Callie.*

With a pucker at his brow, Seth sits up and takes the phone from me. He talks to Callie for about ten minutes and by the time he hangs up, he looks like he's ready to throw up.

"What's wrong?" I ask as he sets my phone down on the nightstand.

"It's Kayden..." Shock is frozen on his face. "He was stabbed this weekend. He's okay, but he's been admitted to the hospital."

"*What?*" I haven't actually met Kayden, but I've gathered from conversations with Seth that Callie really cares about him. "Who the hell stabbed him?"

"I don't know yet, but Callie thinks it might have been his dad," he whispers. "God, Callie told me that Kayden's father was abusive, but I never thought..." His fingers tremble as he balls his hands into fists. "Why do parents have to be so fucked up sometimes?"

"Not all parents are." I reach around and pull him in for a hug. "It's going to be okay."

"I just worry about Callie. She never really breaks down, you know. She just stuffs her emotions until she loses it completely." He inhales and exhales against my chest, trying to pull it together. "I think I need to go there... she shouldn't be alone."

"We can drive out there if you want... I can go with you, too."

"Thank you." The pressure of the last few days becomes too much, causing him to crack, and tears fall from his eyes, dripping onto my shoulder.

Feeling helpless, I do the only thing I can and hold onto him with everything I have in me.

Chapter 14

Greyson

We drove out to be with Callie and to try to see Kayden, but his family wouldn't let anyone in and we ended up going back to the campus. Still, spending time on the road with Seth was nice, even if the trip was for a really depressing reason.

A few weeks pass by and everything seems to be going okay, at least with Seth and me. He's even gotten comfortable enough to occasionally hold my hand in public. I didn't fully grasp how much it bothered me that we couldn't show we're together until he finally decided that he wanted to.

We've reached this nice, comfortable zone of going to school and hanging out. I even got to meet Callie and have been spending a lot of time with her and Seth. The poor girl is completely heartbroken over Kayden. Not only is he still back in his hometown, but he's locked up in a facility because his father told the police that the knife wound to his side was self-inflicted. Apparently, Kayden's been struggling with cutting for a while, so the police believed his father.

"So, what're your plans for Christmas?" Jenna asks as we walk out of the classroom.

It's my last class before winter break begins, and even though I don't hate school, I'm stoked over getting a break. Seth and I are going to spend tonight packing since our flight is tomorrow morning. I'm excited that he's coming with me. I just hope my parents don't overwhelm him.

I sling my bag over my shoulder. "I'm actually going back home with Seth."

"Wow, you guys are getting serious, aren't you?" Jenna says, putting her purple hair into a side braid.

"Yeah, I guess we are." I flatten my palm against the exit door, push it open, and enter the winter storm taking over most of the campus yard. "Actually... I... never mind."

She whirls in front of me, grabbing my arms for support when she almost eats it on the ice. "No way! You have to finish what you were saying."

Seth & Greyson

"It's not that big a deal."

"Yeah, it is. I can tell by the look on your face."

I sigh, drawing my hood over my head. "I was just going to say that I think I'm going to tell Seth I love him while we're in Florida. Out on the beach, maybe at sunset."

"Aw, my Greyson is such a sap." She grins at me as she presses her hand to her chest. "But it's sweet… God, I miss that."

"Miss what?"

"The act of falling in love." Her eyes light up. "That should totally be the name of my next exhibit."

"But you're already in love with Ari." I make a right toward the parking lot, where I'm supposed to meet Seth by his car.

She follows me, making a path around a tree. "I know, but I think I'll make it a goal this holiday to *re*-fall in love with him." Spotting Ari near one of the benches, she gives me a quick kiss on the cheek and skips off toward him. "Wish me luck!"

"Good luck!' I call out then pick up the pace when I see Seth's at his car already, leaning against the hood, waiting for me.

My heart rate quickens as I near him, but the closer I get, the more aware I am that Seth doesn't appear all that happy.

"I have some bad news," he says when I reach him. "I can't go home with you for break."

My good mood crashes. "Why not?"

He motions for me to get into the car. "I'll explain after we get out of the God-awful snow storm." He scowls at the sky then climbs into the car.

I hop in, and he revs the engine before cranking up the heater.

"I need to go home with Callie," he says as he steers the car down the icy road toward my apartment complex. "Kayden hasn't talked to her yet, but he's finally able to have visitors." He flips on the blinker. "I'm worried about her trying to handle that and her family and Caleb all at the same time."

I draw the seatbelt over my shoulder. "Wait... Who's Caleb?"

"The guy who raped her." He turns the wheel and makes a right down the main road.

"Wait. I'm so lost. He's still around?"

Seth & Greyson

"Callie never told her family what happened and, unfortunately, they're pretty clueless about picking up on the fact that their daughter gets extremely uncomfortable every time their son's friend shows up."

"That's so fucked up." I shake my head in disbelief.

"It really is," he agrees, gripping onto the wheel. "Which is why I really need to go home with her. Between her family drama and the fact that Kayden won't even talk to her, she really needs someone there for her." He gives me a sidelong glance. "I hope you're not too mad that I have to cancel on the Florida trip."

"Of course not." I slide my hand across the console and place it on his thigh. "You're a good friend, Seth, and I can't be mad about that."

"I'm going to miss you, though. Like a lot, a lot. Like pour-my-heart-and-soul-out-to-a-diary kind of missing you."

"I'm going to miss you, too." I suddenly realize my grand plans for the big *I love you* reveal just went to shit. "When are you leaving?"

"That's the *really* sucky part. We're catching a ride with Luke, so we have to leave tonight." He pulls the car into the apartment complex, parks in front of my building, and turns in his seat toward me. "You have to promise not to get angry when I text you twenty-four seven. I'm super needy like that."

"I like that you're super needy." I glance around, knowing it's not the beach scene I was planning on, but I've been holding my feelings in far too long already. He needs to know how I feel before we part ways for three weeks. "I have to tell you something. I was actually going to tell you while we were in Florida, but I really just need to get it off my chest." I take an even breath before slipping my fingers through his. "I love you. And I mean, like really fucking love you. I actually have for a while." I sweep my finger along a scar on the back of his hand. "I've never felt this way before." I wait for him to say something, anything, but he remains quiet. "I'm sorry. That was way bad timing, right?"

He nods, a little dazed. "I don't know what to say... I'm just feeling a little overwhelmed."

"You don't have to say anything." I reach for the door handle, feeling more awkward than I ever have in my entire life. "Forget I said it."

Seth & Greyson

"I can't just forget it," he says, looking as though his head is spinning. "It just feels like things are moving super fast... I don't know... I just think I need a break to catch up."

I swallow the lump in my throat. "Well, at least call me when you hit the road, okay? And when you get to Callie's house, too. I want to know you made it there safe." Feeling like I've been punched in the stomach, I shove the door open and climb out of the car.

I don't know why, but I half-expect him to chase after me. Instead, he pulls away, leaving me feeling as though my heart has been ripped out of my chest.

Chapter 15

Seth

I fucked up. Like really, *really* fucked up, worse than I ever have. When Greyson said that he loved me, I freaking panicked and clammed up, my voice catching in my throat as I remembered the last time I uttered those words to a guy.

I love Greyson. Deep down, I think I've known it for a while, just like I know now that I never truly loved Braiden. I fooled myself into believing it was love because he was my first boyfriend. But he wasn't even that, really. Braiden was just a guy I kissed because I thought he was hot.

Yes, Greyson is super fucking hot, but he's so much more than that. *So* much more.

Seth & Greyson

God, what the fuck is wrong with me? I told him I need a break when that's the last damn thing I want. What I *need* is to be with him completely. I'm just so Goddamn scared to open myself up like that again. Everything's moving so fast that I can hardly keep up. First we come so close to having sex, something I've never done before. Then he tells me that he loves me... I feel dizzy just thinking about it all, but a good kind of dizzy. The kind of dizzy that means deep down, I want what he's offering me.

"Seth, please tell me what's bothering you," Callie says, shouting over the music blaring through the club.

We're in San Diego, of all places. I ended up here when Luke, Kayden, Callie, and I all decided to flee their hometown and take a break from... Well, life. Deep down, though, I know I'm here because I'm running away from my problems.

"I'm fine," I assure her, checking my messages for like the hundredth time.

Greyson's hardly texted me since we parted ways, and I don't blame him. The look on his face... God, that look. It's what haunts my dreams at night.

I put my phone into my pocket as Luke leaves the table to go get drinks. I'm dying for a cigarette, but the place is solely no smoking.

Callie wrings her hands on her lap then starts picking at her nails. "Seth, you're not fine."

I take out my phone again, secretly willing Greyson to text me back, but the phone remains silent. "I haven't talked to Greyson since yesterday," I finally give in and divulge. "I think he might be upset with me."

She rests her arms on top of the table. "Why?"

I shrug. "Because I might have said something mean about our relationship."

"Like what?"

"Like I wanted a break." I sigh when she frowns at me in disappointment. "Don't look at me like that. I didn't mean it. I was tired and overthinking things and... I didn't mean it."

She keeps frowning at me the same way. "Did you tell him that?"

"Not yet," I tell her, disappointed in myself. Everything had been going just beautifully and I had to go and fuck it up. All I had to do was open my mouth and speak the truth, something I'm usually good at. But nooo, I had to pick that exact moment to become Speechless Seth. "But I'm working up to an apology."

"Seth." She lays a hand on my arm. "Since when do you hold things in? You should never do that... it's not healthy."

She's sooo quoting me, which I find both amusing and tragic. How can I give all this fantastic advice and refuse to take it myself?

I look at Kayden, who's watching us, before snagging Callie's sleeve and tugging her to her feet. "Come with me for a minute," I say as I drag her to the bathroom, not wanting an audience when I admit what's really going on.

I push through the crowd of people and make my way back to the ladies' room. "Okay, I think I might have messed up," I spill my guts to Callie the moment the door slams shut.

A few woman are primping like divas in front of the mirror, but they're all too drunk to care much that I'm in here

"What happened?" Callie asks, reclining against the sink. "Something with Greyson, I'm guessing."

I nod, rubbing my hand down my face. "I panicked."

"I'm familiar with the term," she says dryly. "But what did you panic about?"

"About—" I lower my voice and move aside as the door swings open and a herd of women come stumbling in. One shoots me a dirty look and I return it before fixing my attention on Callie again. "About our relationship."

"Your's and Greyson's?"

"Yeah, I think I'm having flashbacks."

The women around us are being nosy little biotches, so I grab Callie's hand and pull her into the handicapped stall. Locking the door, I let go of her arm and rake my fingers through my hair, deciding exactly how much I should tell her.

"Seth, whatever it is, please just tell me," she pleads. "You know you can tell me anything."

I pull a wary face, knowing I'm about to make her uncomfortable. "It's about intimacy."

She squirms, just like I knew she would. "I can handle it."

"Are you sure?"

She steps forward, squaring her shoulders. "Yes, I'm your best friend and you can tell me anything."

Sighing, I pace the length of the stall, restless. "I can't go through with it…and not because I'm worried about finally going that far. It's because I keep having flashbacks."

"About what?"

I stop pacing. "Of Braiden."

"Do you still have feelings for him?" she asks, picking at the latch on the stall.

"No, it's not that..." I shake my head, trying to get my thoughts and emotions together. "It's…it's about getting my heart broken."

"It's going to be okay." She inches toward me and touches my arm. "Greyson's *not* Braiden."

"I know that." I place my hand over hers. "But sometimes, I find myself going back to that place where I'm lying in the dirt and they're kicking the shit out of me."

She pulls me in for one of her teddy-bear hugs. "I know, but sometimes moving forward is the only way we can escape our pasts, right? At least that's what you're always telling me."

"I know," I whisper, pulling her closer. "And I know nothing bad will happen. Greyson's not Braiden and he... loves me, but I just keep thinking about that Goddamn day. I was so fucking happy, thinking life was perfect, and then they showed up, all piled into the back of that fucking truck like a bunch of robots following what the other one does. And..." Tears sting in my eyes. "And I can't stop picturing his face—the hate in his eyes, like he was blaming me for being part of it. I thought I was over it after seeing him on Thanksgiving, but sometimes it sneaks back up on me during the worst fucking times." Like when Greyson decided to tell me that he loves me.

I pull back, drying the tears with the back of my hand. "Anyway, what I was going to say before I started bawling like a baby was that I was feeling a little scared about moving forward and I might have said some things to Greyson that weren't very nice."

"You could try apologizing." She tears off some tissue from the roll and hands it to me. "Sometimes saying sorry is easy."

I dab my eyes then chuck the tissue into the garbage. "Yeah, but sometimes it's not. I've tried to say it quite a few times since we've been apart, but it never comes out right."

"But sometimes it is," she says determinedly, being her little sparkler self.

I can't help but smile. "Look at you, being all wise." I slip my arm around her shoulder. "I think it must be from all the time you've spent around me."

She cracks a smile as she unlocks the stall. "It must be."

We leave the bathroom and go back to the table to drink, but I barely pay attention to anything going on around me. My thoughts are stuck on Greyson and what I need to say to him to make things right.

I think I know. I just hope he'll give me a chance to say it.

Chapter 16

Seth

After a very dramatic weekend wherein Kayden bailed on us to go fix his life, Luke, Callie, and I returned to their hometown and rented a hotel room. Callie is pretending that Kayden leaving isn't bothering her, but I can tell it is. I've tried to talk to her a few times, but she's refusing to admit how upset she is.

After I change into my pajamas, I check my phone for a message from Greyson. I haven't heard a peep from him in over two days, and I'm starting to get really worried he might have given up on me. The idea shatters my heart, and the pain is worse than anything I've ever felt. I need it to go away, like now.

Before I can back out, I lock myself in the bathroom and dial his number. "Please, pick up. Please, pick up," I chant as I lower myself to the floor.

Seth & Greyson

When he doesn't answer, I decide to leave a brief message that will hopefully get him to call me back.

"Hey, it's Seth." I roll my eyes at myself and sigh. "Look, I know you're upset with me and I get it. You have every right to be, but I really need to talk to you, like super badly. And I…. I know I don't deserve this, but I still haven't collected on my winnings for that poker game, and this is the one thing I want. For you to call me. So please, *please,* just call me back."

I hang up and clutch the phone in my hand. One minute later, the ringer goes off, scaring the living daylights out of me.

"Hey," I hurry and answer, sounding a bit breathless.

"Hello." Even though he sounds a bit upset, I instantly relax at the sound of his voice.

"I love you," I blurt out before I chicken out. All the baggage I've been carrying around suddenly feels so much lighter. "Oh, this is Seth, by the way."

There's a pause and then he laughs. It's the most wonderful sound in the fucking world. Seriously, music to my ears.

"I know who it is," he says, sounding less tense than when he answered. "You said so on your message. I don't know why, though. It's not like I deleted your number from my phone or something."

"But you thought about it."

"I did a couple of times, but couldn't bring myself to do it... To erase you from my life like that." He pauses again. "Do you really mean it?"

"That I love you..." I bite on my fingernail. "I really fucking do. I mean it more than I've ever meant anything."

"I love you, too."

"Obviously. I'm me, aren't I?" I joke, but there's nothing funny about the situation. Not at all. "I'm sorry I didn't say it back at your place... I just panicked and I don't know... I just needed some time to sort through all the bad crap to get to the good."

"God, I've missed you," he says. "I wish you were here with me so I could kiss you or something."

I lean against the door and stretch my legs out. "I wish you were here, too. The good news is that we'll be back home in four days. Then you can kiss me all you want."

"Oh, I plan on it," he says matter-of-factly.

Seth & Greyson

My stomach does that ridiculous dance again as I think about *being* with him. Yes, I'm afraid, but the only way to get past the fear is to face it. And there's nothing I want more than to be with Greyson.

By the time we've finished talking, it's well after midnight. When I exit the bathroom, brushing my teeth, Callie's in bed and Luke's outside smoking.

Callie gives me a strange look. "Something happened."

I pull the toothbrush out of my mouth, unable to contain my grin. "I called Greyson," I declare with a mouth full of toothpaste.

"Did you work everything out?" she asks, fluffing her pillow.

Nodding, I head to the bathroom, spitting in the sink and rinsing my toothbrush before returning to the room and climbing into bed with her.

"I told him I loved him," I say after I pull the covers over me.

"You love him?" Callie pushes up on her elbow and stares down at me. "You never told me that?"

"I know… But I do. Like a lot, a lot."

Jessica Sorensen

"And what did he say?"

"I love you, too," I grin like a silly nut job.

"Seth, I'm really happy for you."

"I'm really happy for me, too."

Still smiling, I roll over and close my eyes. I realize there's still a lot of stuff I have to deal with, but knowing I have Greyson there to help me makes it easier to face.

Chapter 17

Greyson

I don't think I've ever been so fucking excited to see someone as I am now. Seth and I made plans for him to pick me up at the airport. By the time I walk out of the door, dragging my suitcase behind me, it's past ten o'clock. The winter air instantaneously stings my lightly sun-kissed skin. Shivering, I search the pick-up area for Seth and spot him leaning against his car just to my right.

A smile spreads across his face as soon as he sees me and it takes all of my effort not to drop my bag and kiss him right here in the midst of hundreds of post-holiday travelers. The only thing stopping me is the caution in his eyes. We're still not in the same place yet, which is okay. He has a lot of stuff to deal with, but at least he's working on it instead of running away.

"Hey," I say, stopping in front of him.

Jessica Sorensen

He smiles at me, takes my bag, and tosses it into the backseat. Without saying a word, he rounds the back of the car, opens the driver's door, and climbs in. I follow his lead and slide into the passenger seat. The moment I get the door shut, he reaches over, cups the back of my neck, and pulls my mouth to his.

"God, I missed you," I murmur as I taste his lips.

"Me, too," he agrees, his fingers fumbling as he grips onto my arms. "Just FYI, we're *so* spending spring break together."

"Works for me. I hated being apart." I lean back and buckle my seatbelt as he drives down the ramp toward the road. "How did everything go on your trip?"

He taps the breaks, bringing the car to a stop at a streetlight. "Well, there was a lot of drama, none of which I caused, surprisingly."

"With Callie and Kayden, I'm guessing?"

He nods. "But I think," he holds up his hands with his fingers crossed, "they might finally have worked it out. She even told her parents what Caleb did to her."

"Wow, that was really brave of her."

212

"It really was." He drives forward when the light turns green. "I think they handled it pretty well, too, which restores my faith a little in parents."

"Not all parents are bad. And speaking of parents." I reach into my pocket and dig out a bracelet my mother sent Seth. "My mom wanted me to give this to you." I hand him the bracelet and he stares at it, his forehead creased. "I know it's tacky and definitely not your style, but there's four leaf clovers woven in the shells that are supposed to bring you luck or strength." I shrug. "I'm not really sure which, because sometimes I zone out when she starts rambling about herbs and karma and auras, but she said something about wanting to give you some of her luck because you deserve it. And that every time you look at it, she wants you to remember how strong you are."

He grins from ear to ear as he clasps the bracelet in his hand. "I seriously can't wait to meet your mother."

"You don't have to wear it if you don't want to."

"No, I want to." To prove it, he slips it onto his wrist.

We make the rest of the drive holding hands and don't let go as we walk up the stairs to my apartment. I unlock the door one handed, and the moment I step inside and kick the door shut, Seth's mouth is devouring mine.

I drop my bag somewhere on the floor, not bothering to turn on the lights as we stumble back to my bedroom. We only break the kiss long enough to pull off our shirts and jeans, reconnecting as we fall onto the bed. The kiss is slow, my tongue inspecting every inch of his mouth as he does the same to mine.

I support my weight on my arms as I roll on top of him, breathing heavily. "We can go slow…" I trail off as he slips his hand down the front of my boxers, gripping me firmly.

My cock jerks with need and I'm seriously about to fucking lose it before we even get started.

He swallows nervously and shakes his head. "No. No more Ferris Wheel."

I can't help myself. Laughter erupts from my chest.

He grins proudly. "That really was a good one, wasn't it? And I didn't even plan it."

I shake my head, still laughing a little, but the laughter swiftly fades as he starts moving his hand up and down.

I struggle to breathe, needing to know, "Are you *sure* you're sure? I promise we don't have to do this now… I know you've had to deal with a lot lately. I don't want to push you into anything."

"Greyson, I'm sure. Trust me. I'm more sure about this than anything else." Then he pushes up on his elbow and seals his lips to mine.

Chapter 18

Seth

I hate that I'm still afraid. For a moment, I put up my walls and fall straight into my usual defense mechanism, cracking some absurdly inappropriately timed joke about Ferris Wheels. Still, it gets Greyson to laugh and helps me breathe just a little bit easier.

We start off slow, allowing our hands and mouths to search each other's bodies. His skin is so soft, his body so amazing, and he tastes like mint and chocolate, completely delicious. I get lost in it. *Him.* Everything that is him. Nothing about the situation is funny, and I don't want it to be.

My nerves start to get the best of me when he rolls the condom down his length, but then he kisses me and everything is okay. Just. Like. That.

Seth & Greyson

"Are you sure?" Greyson checks for the millionth time, simply because that's the kind of guy he is.

He's the guy who always makes sure I'm okay, who is by far the most patient person I've ever met, who makes me feel safe, and who puts my needs before his own. Of course, because I'm the slightest bit vain, I have to add how incredibly sexy he is to the list.

Since I'm nervous beyond belief, I open my mouth to tease him about asking me again, but not wanting to ruin the moment, I decide just to nod. "I love you."

His lips tug to a lopsided grin. "I love you, too."

Greyson spent a long time preparing me and once he's inside me, I wonder what I was so afraid of to begin with. It's better than I ever imagined, completely opposite of the one-sided fumbling I experienced before. It's a perfect balance of give and take and give and take as he grips me in his hand, rocking into me while I kiss him with all the pent up desire I have in me. We completely lose it together, kissing all the way to the end.

Greyson climbs off of me, cleaning both of us before we lie down in bed together wrapped in each other's arms. It remains silent for a while, the soft moonlight trailing through the window and across his face.

"What are you thinking about?" I ask as I slide my knee between his legs.

"Something my mom said." He turns his head, slides his hand around the back of my neck, and plays with the hair at my nape. "She made this prediction that I was going to meet someone while I was here."

"So, you believe her now about being psychic?" I ask as he slips his other arm under my head.

"No, I think us being together… that was all us. Yeah, it hasn't been easy, but it's worth it."

"Yeah, it is." I stare at the bracelet he gave me. The thing is hideous, but what it represents is the most beautiful thing in the world. Every time I look at it, I'll remember that not all the world is ugly and full of hate. That there are people out there who firmly believe that no one should ever be afraid to love. That love is simply love, and that regardless of the form in which it arrives, that there's beauty in it all. "I'm going to try to do better. I know it might take me a while to completely be myself in front of everyone, but I promise I'll get there."

"I know you will. And you want to know why?" He grazes his fingers along the scars on my arm. "Because you're seriously the fucking strongest person I've ever met."

"I wouldn't go that far. Just wait until you try to get me to exercise, then you'll realize how weak I am." He shakes his head and I smile. "I'm kidding. Seriously, thank you for saying that. It means a lot."

We kiss until we fall asleep in each other's arms, and I drift into the most peaceful dreams I've had in a long time.

Chapter 19

Three weeks later…

Seth

For once in my life, I actually feel like I'm being myself. Now that I'm not so afraid, I've started opening up more. Sure, I still crack jokes sometimes to cover up my feelings, just like I sprinkle my flamboyant opinions wherever I see fit.

Greyson and I are officially together and a lot of people know about it. Yes, it's terrifying when someone makes some snide comment or stares at us when we're holding hands, but I've mostly felt the love, more than I thought I ever would. And no matter what happens, Greyson, Callie, and, yes, even Luke and Kayden have been super supportive.

Seth & Greyson

I've even decided to start dipping my toe into the world of sports. Granted, I find it rather boring, but Greyson seems into it, which is enough for me to go sit on the bleachers and pretend not to smell the stench of sweat that seems to permeate the air whenever anything athletic is involved.

Right now, I'm at a basketball game with Greyson, Luke, and Callie. The crowd is going crazy, whistling and screaming and about as wild and out of control as Jenna is when she eats too much cotton candy.

"Where are Greyson and Luke?" Callie asks as she plops down on the bench beside me.

I point out Luke and Greyson in the bottom row in our section. Greyson keeps waving his arms around, his eyes lighting up the way they always do when he's talking about something that excites him. Luke is shaking his head in disagreement and sticking his hands out to the side. More than likely, they're discussing either photography or the gym, both of which I find a little boring, but I love watching Greyson debate things he's passionate about.

I reach into the popcorn bucket and stuff a handful into my mouth. "What's with the silly grin, my darling Callie?"

She sticks her hand into the bucket. "Kayden just told me he loves me."

I almost throw the popcorn bucket onto the bald guy's head in front of us. "I'm so happy for you," I say as I grab her and pull her in for a hug.

She folds her arms around me. "I'm really happy for me, too."

I pull away and set the popcorn bucket onto the floor. "I know you are, which is good. I really didn't want to kick Kayden's ass."

She laughs at that. "I'm sure Kayden's grateful, too."

A large man behind us starts yelling at Luke and Greyson to "sit the fuck down!"

Feeling like the protective boyfriend, I turn around and yell, "Shut the hell up," while Luke flips him the middle finger.

Seriously, sports fans are insane.

Seth & Greyson

Grabbing the bucket of popcorn, I fix my attention back on Callie, only to find her staring at Luke.

"Sometimes…I wonder if Luke…" She leans in and whispers, "If Luke…likes… guys."

I almost choke on my popcorn. "Luke's not gay, Callie."

"Are you sure? Maybe he's just afraid to come out, like Braiden was."

"Yeah, I'm sure." I glance down at Greyson and Luke, shaking my head. "You want to know what I think?"

She nods, stealing a handful of popcorn. "Yes, please share your knowledge, Oh Wise One."

I scoot closer to her. "I think that Luke's been through something that makes him more understanding and accepting than the average person. And I think that sometimes people misinterpret understanding and acceptance and make it into something that it isn't."

"You're right and I'm sorry," she says with a trace of embarrassment. "I should never assume things about people."

"You don't need to apologize." I playfully poke her in the side. "Besides, you're one of those people."

"What? Understanding and accepting?"

"The kind of person who sees things in a different light because they've been to hell and back. The kind who has given and received redemption."

We exchange a smile as the crowd goes berserk, shouting and clapping and jumping up from their seats. I start clapping, too, even though I have no damn clue what's going on.

Callie's phone rings and she shouts, "It's my brother!" She jumps to her feet with her phone in her hand. "I'll be right back. He's been trying to call me all night."

She hurries down the stairs and I turn my attention back to Greyson and Luke, thinking about going down there and joining them, but they're already climbing the stairs toward me.

Luke takes a seat down at the end of the bench where Callie was sitting, and Greyson sits beside me.

"Having fun?" he asks, grabbing a handful of popcorn from the bucket.

Seth & Greyson

"Oh, yeah, a *blast*." I smirk. "You so owe me for this one."

He grins as he shoves his mouth full of popcorn. "Sounds good to me." As the people in the bleachers continue bouncing and screaming at the game, he leans in and whispers, "Thank you for coming with me."

I slide my hand toward his and lace our fingers. My heart pumps deafeningly from inside my chest, but I refuse to pull away. He smiles at me and I take a deep breath, feeling my scars become less visible. Sure, the ones on my arm are still there, and they always will be. But the ones on the inside, those are the ones I have control over. And I know as long as I stay strong, they'll continue to fade away.

Jessica Sorensen

Seth & Greyson

Jessica Sorensen

Seth & Greyson

About the Author

Jessica Sorensen is a *New York Times* and *USA Today* bestselling author that lives in the snowy mountains of Wyoming. When she's not writing, she spends her time reading and hanging out with her family.

Other books by Jessica Sorensen:

<u>The Coincidence Series:</u>

The Coincidence of Callie and Kayden

The Redemption of Callie and Kayden

The Destiny of Violet and Luke

The Probability of Violet and Luke

The Certainty of Violet and Luke

The Resolution of Callie and Kayden

Seth & Greyson

Jessica Sorensen

The Secret Series:

The Prelude of Ella and Micha

The Secret of Ella and Micha

The Forever of Ella and Micha

The Temptation of Lila and Ethan

The Ever After of Ella and Micha

Lila and Ethan: Forever and Always

Ella and Micha: Infinitely and Always

The Shattered Promises Series:

Shattered Promises

Fractured Souls

Unbroken

Broken Visions

Scattered Ashes (Coming Soon)

Breaking Nova Series:

Breaking Nova

Seth & Greyson

Saving Quinton

Delilah: The Making of Red

Nova and Quinton: No Regrets

Tristan: Finding Hope

Wreck Me

Ruin Me

The Fallen Star Series (YA):

The Fallen Star

The Underworld

The Vision

The Promise

The Fallen Souls Series (spin off from The Fallen Star):

The Lost Soul

The Evanescence

The Darkness Falls Series:

Darkness Falls

Darkness Breaks

Darkness Fades

The Death Collectors Series (NA and YA):

Ember X and Ember

Cinder X and Cinder

Spark X and Cinder (Coming Soon)

The Sins Series:

Seduction & Temptation

Sins & Secrets

Unbeautiful Series:

Unbeautiful

Untamed

Seth & Greyson

Jessica Sorensen

CPSIA information can be obtained at www.ICGtesting.com
Printed in the USA
LVOW07s1821070715

445305LV00005B/383/P